TABLOID
DREAMS

TABLOID DREAMS

stories

Robert Olen Butler

Grove Press
New York

First published in the United States of America by Henry Holt and Company, Inc., 1996

Published simultaneously in Canada
Printed in the United States of America

ISBN-13: 978-0-8021-2098-4

Grove Press
an imprint of Grove/Atlantic, Inc.
841 Broadway
New York, NY 10003

Distributed by Publishers Group West

www.groveatlantic.com

13 14 15 16   10 9 8 7 6 5 4 3 2 1

For Allen H. Peacock, my friend
and my editor for the crucial decade

And for my wife, Kelly, who makes
all things possible

Contents

The stories in this book first appeared in the following places: "*Titanic* Victim Speaks Through Waterbed," *Missouri Review;* "Woman Uses Glass Eye to Spy on Philandering Husband," *Mississippi Review Web;* "Boy Born with Tattoo of Elvis," *Conjunctions;* "Woman Loses Cookie Bake-Off, Sets Self on Fire," *The Gettysburg Review;* "Jealous Husband Returns in Form of Parrot," *The New Yorker;* "Woman Struck by Car Turns into Nymphomaniac," *Mississippi Review Web;* "Nine-Year-Old Boy Is World's Youngest Hit Man," *The Southern Review;* "Every Man She Kisses Dies," *Mānoa: A Pacific Journal of International Writing;* "Doomsday Meteor Is Coming," *Literal Latté;* "Help Me Find My Spaceman Lover," *The Paris Review;* "JFK Secretly Attends Jackie Auction," *Esquire* (under the title "The Auction"); "*Titanic* Survivors Found in Bermuda Triangle," *Colorado Review*.

"*Titanic* Victim Speaks Through Waterbed"

This is a bit of a puzzle, really. A certain thrashing about overhead. Swimmers with nowhere to go, I fear, though I don't recognize this body of water. I've grown quite used to this existence I now have. I'm fully conscious that I'm dead. And yet not so, somehow. I drift and drift, and I am that in which I drift, though what that is now, precisely, is unclear to me. There was darkness at first, and I failed to understand. But then I rose as some faint current from the depths of the North Atlantic and there were others around me, the corporeal creatures of the sea whom I had hitherto known strictly on fine china and dressed lightly in butter and lemon. I found that I was the very medium for the movement of their piscine limbs, and they seemed oblivious to my consciousness. Given their ignorance, I could not even haunt them. But I understood, by then, of what my fundamental state consisted, something that had eluded the wisdom of Canterbury. Something for which I was unprepared.

And after many years—I don't know how many, but it is clear to me that it is not an inconsiderable sum—there are still surprises awaiting me. This impulse now to shape words, for instance. And the thrashing above me, the agitation it brings upon me. I returned to the first-class smoking lounge soon after I realized what had happened to the ship. I sat in an overstuffed leather chair and then looked about for a dry match to light my cigar. But I was well aware of what was going on out in the darkness beyond the window.

Perhaps that accounts for the slight betrayal of fear, something only I could notice, since on the surface I seemed to be in control: I sat down and reached for a match. But I sat down already fearing that the matches would be wet. I should have searched for the match and then sat down. But I sat. And then I looked about. And, of course, the room was quite dry. On the table, just at arm's length, was a silver-plated ashtray with a silver matchbox engraved with the flag of the White Star Line rising on a pedestal from its center. The box was full of matches. I took one and struck it and it flared into life and I held it to my cigar and I thought, What a shame that this quite charming ashtray will be soon lost. My hand was steady. To anyone watching, it would seem I had never doubted that the matches in this room were dry. Of course they were. At that hour the ship was beginning to settle into the water, but only like a stout fellow standing in this very room after a long night of cards and feeling heavy in his lower limbs. It was, of course, impossible for water to be in this room as yet. That would come only very near the end. But still I feared that the matches would already be spoilt.

All through that night, the fear was never physical. I didn't mind so much, in point of fact, giving up a life in my body. The body was never a terribly interesting thing to me. Except perhaps to draw in the heavy curl of the smoke of my cigar, like a Hindu's rope in the market rising as if it were a thing alive. One needs a body to smoke a good cigar. I took the first draw there in that room just below the fourth funnel of the largest ship in the world as it sat dead still, filling with the North Atlantic ocean in the middle of the night, and the smoke was a splendid thing.

And as I did, I felt an issue of perspiration on my forehead. This was not unpleasant, however. I sat with many a fine cigar on the verandah of my bungalow in Madras, and though one of the boys was always there to fan the punkah, I would perspire on my forehead and it was just part of smoking a good cigar out in India. With a whisky and soda beside me. I thought, sitting on the sinking ship, about pouring myself a drink. But I didn't. I wanted a clear head. I had gone to my cabin when things seemed serious and I'd changed into evening dress. It was a public event, it seemed to me. It was a solemn occasion. With, I assumed, a King to meet somewhat higher even than our good King George. I didn't feel comfortable in tweeds.

What *is* that thrashing about above me now? The creatures of the sea are absent here, though I'm not risen into the air as I have done for some years, over and over, lifted and dispersed into cloud. I'm coalesced in a place that has no living creatures but is large enough for me to be unable quite to sense its boundaries. Perhaps not too large, since I am not moving except for a faint eddying from the activity above. But at least I am in a place larger than a teacup. I once dwelt in a cup of tea, and on that occasion, I sensed the constraints of the space.

I yearn to be clothed now in the evening dress I wore on that Sunday night in April in the year of 1912. I must say that a body is useful for formal occasions, as well. All this floating about seems much too casual to me. I expected something more rigorous in the afterlife. A propitiatory formality. A sensible accounting. Order. But there has been no sign, as yet, of that King of Kings. Just this long and elemental passage to a place I cannot recognize. And an odd sense of alertness now. And these words I feel compelled to speak.

There. I think I heard the sound of a human voice above me in this strange place. Very briefly. I cannot make out the words, if words this voice indeed uttered. It's been a rare thing for me, in all this time, to sense that a living human being might be close by. On that dark night in the North Atlantic, at the very moment we struck our fate out somewhere beneath the water line on our bow, I was in the midst of voices that did not resolve themselves into clear words, and none of us heard anything of that fateful event. I was sitting and smoking, and there was a voluble conversation over a card game near to me. It was late. Nearly midnight. I was reluctant to leave the company of these men, though I had not said more than two dozen words to any of them on this night, beyond "good evening." I am an indifferent card player. I sat and smoked all evening and I missed having the latest newspaper. I don't remember what I might have thought about, with all that smoke. India perhaps. Perhaps my sister and her husband in Toronto, towards whom we had just ceased to steam.

What did become clear to me quite quickly was that we had stopped. I looked at the others and they were continuing to play their game unaware of anything unusual. So I rose and stepped out under the wrought-iron and glass dome of the aft staircase. I had no apprehensions. The staircase was very elegant with polished oak wall paneling and gilt on the balustrades and it was lit bright with electric lights. My feeling was that in the absence of the threat of native rebellion, things such as this could not possibly be in peril.

That seems a bit naive now, of course, but at the time, I was straight from the leather chair of the first-class smoking lounge. And I was tutored in my views by the Civil Service in India. And I was a keen reader of the newspapers and all that they had to say about this new age of technology, an age for which this unsinkable ship stood as eloquent testament. And I was an old bachelor whose only sister lived in the safest dominion of the empire.

Owing to the lateness of the hour, there was no one about on the staircase except for a steward who rushed past me and down the steps. "What's the trouble?" I asked him.

He waved a hot water bottle he was carrying and said, "Cold feet, I presume," and he disappeared on the lower landing.

I almost stepped back into the smoking lounge. But there was no doubt that we had come to a full stop, and that was unquestionably out of the ordinary. Two or three of the card players were now standing in the doorway just behind me, murmuring about this very thing.

"I'll see what's the matter," I said without looking at them, and I descended the steps and went out onto the open promenade.

The night was very still. There were people moving about, somewhat distractedly, but I paid them no attention. I stepped to the railing and the sea was vast and smooth in the moonlight. There were shapes out there, like water buffalo sleeping in the fields in the dark nights outside Madras. I would drive back to my bungalow in a trap, my head still cluttered with the talk and the music from the little dance band and the whirling around of the dancers, and I would think how the social rites of my own class sometimes felt as foreign to me as those of the people we were governing here. These pretenses the men and women made in order to touch, often someone else's spouse. I am not unobservant. But I would go to these events, nevertheless. Even if I kept to myself.

I looked out at these sleeping shapes in the water. A woman's voice was suddenly nearby.

"We're doomed now," she said in the flat inflection of an American.

It took a moment to realize that she was addressing me. She said no more. But I think I heard her breathing. I turned and she was less than an arm's length from me along the railing. In the brightness of the moon I could see her face quite clearly. She seemed rather young, though less than two hours later I would revise that somewhat. The first impression, however, was that she was young, and that was all. Perhaps rather pretty, too, but I don't think I noticed that at the time. There were certain things that I suppose were beyond my powers of observation. When I realized to whom she was speaking, her words finally registered on me.

"Not at all." I spoke from whatever ignorance I had learned all my life. "Nothing that can't be handled. This is a fine ship."

"I'm not in a panic," she said. "You can hear that in my voice, can't you?"

"Of course."

"I just know this terrible thing to be true."

I leaned on the rail and looked at these sleeping cattle. I knew what they were. I understood what this woman had concluded. "It's the ice you fear," I said.

"The deed is done, don't you think?" she said.

Her breath puffed out, white in the moonlight, and I felt suddenly responsible for her. There was nothing personal in it. But this was a lady in some peril, I realized. At least in peril from her own fears. I felt a familiar stiffening in me, and I was glad of it. Dissipated now were the effects of the cigar smoke and the comfort of a chair in a place where men gathered in their complacent ease. But I still felt I only needed to dispel some groundless fears of a woman too much given to her intuition.

"What deed might that be?" I asked her, trying to gentle my voice.

"We've struck an iceberg."

I was surprised to find that this seemed entirely plausible. "And suppose we have," I said. "This ship is the very most modern afloat. The watertight compartments make it quite unsinkable. We would, perhaps, at worst, be delayed."

She turned her face to me, though she did not respond.

"Are you traveling alone?" I asked.

"Yes."

"Perhaps that accounts for your anxiety."

"No. It was the deep and distant sound of the collision. And the vibration I felt in my feet. And the speed with which we were hurtling among these things." She nodded to the shapes in the dark. I looked and felt a chill from the night air. "And the dead stop we instantly made," she said. "And it's a thing in the air. I can smell it. A thing that I smelled once before, when I was a little girl. A coal mine collapsed in my hometown. Many men were trapped and would die within a few hours. I smell that again . . . These are the things that account for my anxiety."

"You shouldn't be traveling alone," I said. "If I might say so."

"No, you might not say so," she said, and she turned her face sharply to the sea.

"I'm sorry," I said. Though I felt I was right. A woman alone could be subject to torments of the sensibility such as this and have no one to comfort her. I wanted to comfort this woman beside me.

Is this an eddy through what once was my mind? A stirring of the water in which I'm held? I ripple and suddenly

I see this clearly: my wish to comfort her came from an impulse stronger than duty would strictly require. I see this now, dissolved as I have been for countless years in the thing that frightened her that night. But standing with her at the rail, I simply wished for a companion to comfort her on a troubling night, a father or a brother perhaps.

"You no doubt mean well," she said.

"Yes. Of course."

"I believe a woman should vote too," she said.

"Quite," I said. This was a notion I'd heard before and normally it seemed, in the voice of a woman, a hard and angry thing. But now this woman's voice was very small. She was arguing her right to travel alone and vote when, in fact, she feared she would soon die in the North Atlantic Ocean. I understood this much and her words did not seem provocative to me. Only sad.

"I'm certain you'll have a chance to express that view for many decades to come," I said.

"The change is nearer than you think," she said with some vigor now in her voice, even irritation. I was glad to hear it.

"I didn't mean to take up the political point," I said. "I simply meant you will survive this night and live a long time."

She lowered her face.

"That's your immediate concern, isn't it?" I asked, trying to speak very gently.

Before she could answer, a man I knew from the smoking lounge approached along the promenade, coming from the direction of the bow of the ship. He had gone out of the lounge some time earlier.

"Look here," he said, and he showed me his drink. It was full of chipped ice. "It's from the forward well deck," he said. "It's all over the place."

I felt the woman ease around my shoulder and look into the glass. The man was clearly drunk and shouldn't have been running about causing alarm.

"From the iceberg," he said.

I heard her exhale sharply.

"I never take ice in my scotch and soda," I said.

The man drew himself up. "I do," he said. And he moved away unsteadily, confirming my criticism of him.

She stood very still for a long moment.

All I could think to say was something along the lines of "Here, here. There's nothing to worry about." But she was not the type of woman to take comfort from that. I knew that much about her already. I felt no resentment at the fact. Indeed, I felt sorry for her. If she wanted to be the sort to travel alone and vote and not be consoled by the platitudes of a stiff old bachelor from the Civil Service in India, then it was sad for her to have these intense and daunting intuitions of disaster and death, as well.

So I kept quiet, and she eventually turned her face to me. The moon fell upon her. At the time, I did not clearly see her beauty. I can see it now, however. I have always been able to see in this incorporeal state. Quite vividly. Though not at the moment. There's only darkness. The activity above me has no shape. But in the sea, as I drifted inexorably to the surface, I began to see the fish and eventually the ceiling of light above me. And then there was the first time I rose—quite remarkable—lifting from the vastness of an ocean delicately wrinkled and athrash with the sunlight. I went up into a sky I knew I was a part of, spinning myself into the gossamer of a rain cloud, hiding from the sea, traced as a tiny wisp into a great gray mountain of vapor. And I wondered if there were others like me there. I listened for them. I tried to call to them, though I had no voice. Not even words. Not like these that now shape in me. If I'd had these words then, perhaps I could have called out to the others who had gone down with the *Titanic*, and they would have heard me. If, in fact, they were there. But as far as I knew—as far as I know now—I am a solitary traveler.

And then I was rain, and the cycle began. And I moved in the clouds and in the tides and eventually I became rivers and streams and lakes and dew and a cup of tea. Darjeeling. In a place not unlike the one where I spent so many years. I had recently come out of the sea, but I don't think the place was Madras or near it, for the sea must have been the Arabian, not the Bay of Bengal. I was in a reservoir and then in a well and then in a boiling kettle and eventually in a porcelain cup, very thin: I could see the shadow of a woman's hand pick me up. I sensed it was Darjeeling tea, but I don't know how. Perhaps I can smell, too, in this state, but without the usual body, perhaps there is only the knowledge of the scent. I'm not sure. But I slipped inside a woman and then later I was—how shall I say this?—free again. I must emphasize that I kept my spirit's eyes tightly shut.

That was many years ago. I subsequently crossed the subcontinent and then Indochina and then I spent a very long time in another vast sea, the Pacific Ocean, I'm sure. And then, in recent times, I rolled in a storm front across a rough coast and rained hard in a new land. I think, in fact, I have arrived in the very country for which I'd set sail in that fateful spring of 1912.

Her country. I'm digressing now. I see that. I look at her face in this memory that drifts with me—I presume forever—and I am ready to understand that she was beautiful, from the first, and I look away, just as I did then. I talk of everything but her face. She turned to me and the moon fell upon her and I could not bring myself to be the pompous ass I am capable of being. I said nothing to reassure her. And that was an act of respect. I see that now. I wonder if she saw it. But neither did I say anything else. I looked away. I looked out to the sea that was even then trying to claim us both, and I finally realized she was gone.

She had said nothing more, either. Not good-bye. Nothing. Not that I blame her. I'd let her down somehow. And she knew that we were all in mortal peril. When I turned back around and found her gone, I had a feeling about her absence. A feeling that I quickly set aside. It had something to do with my body. I felt a chill. But, of course, we were in the North Atlantic with ice floating all about us. I wished I were in my bungalow near the Bay of Bengal, wrapped in mosquito netting and drifting into unconsciousness. I wished for that, at the time. I did not wish for her to return. I wanted only to be lying in a bed alone in a place I knew very well, a place where I could spend my days being as stiff as I needed to be to keep going. I wanted to lie wrapped tight, with the taste of cigars and whisky still faint in my mouth, and sleep.

And now I feel something quite strong, really. Though I have no body, whatever I am feels suddenly quite profoundly empty. Ah empty. Ah quite quite empty.

I have cried out. Just now. And the thrashing above me stops and turns into a low murmur of voices. The water moves, a sharp undulation, and then suddenly there's a faint light above me. I had rushed through dark tunnels into this place and had no idea what it was, and now I can see it is structured and tight. The light is a square ceiling above me. I see it through the water, but there is something else, as well, blurring the light. Mosquito netting. A shroud. Something. It is quite odd, really.

I want to think on this place I'm in, but I cannot. There's only the empty space on the promenade where she'd stood. I turned and she was gone and I looked both ways and there were people moving about, but I did not see her. It was then that I knew for certain that she was right. I knew the ship would go down, and I would die.

So I went to my cabin and closed the door and laid out my evening clothes on the bed. There were footsteps in the hallway, racing. Others knew. I imagined her moving about the ship like some Hindu spirit taken human form, visiting this truth upon whomever would listen. I once again stood still for a moment with a feeling. I wanted her to have spoken only to me. That we should keep that understanding strictly between the two of us. I straightened now and put the thought from my head. That thought, not the sinking of the ship, made me quake slightly inside. I straightened and stiffened with as much reserve and dignity as possible for a man in late middle age standing in his underwear, and I carefully dressed for this terrible event.

When I came out again on the promenade deck, I hesitated. But only briefly. Something very old and very strong in me brought me to the door of the smoking lounge. This was the only place that seemed familiar to me, that was filled with people whose salient qualities I could recognize easily.

I stepped in and the card game was still on. Several faces turned to me.

"It's all up for us," I said, matter-of-factly.

"Yes," one of them said.

"You can bet rather more freely," I said to him.

"Don't encourage him," said another at the table.

"Right," I said. Then I stood there for a moment. I knew that I'd come to join them. My chair sat empty near the card table. And I began to worry about finding a dry match. Force of habit—no, not habit; the indomitable instinct of my life—moved me into the room and to the chair and I sat and I worried about the matches and then I found that they were dry and I lit my cigar and I took a puff and I thought about getting a drink and I thought about meeting a King more powerful than King George and then I suddenly turned away from all that. I laid my cigar in the silver-plate ashtray and I rose and went out of the lounge.

It took me the better part of an hour to find her. At first, things were civilized. They were beginning to put women and children into the boats and people were keeping their heads about them. These were first-class passengers and I moved through them and we all of us exchanged careful apologies for being in each other's way or asking each other to move. With each exchanged request for pardon, I grew more concerned. From this very sharing of the grace of daily human affairs, I responded more and more to the contrast of the situation. I could tell there weren't enough lifeboats for this enterprise. Any fool could tell that. I searched these faces to whom I gently offered my apologies and who gently returned them, but I was not gentle inside. I wanted to find her. I prayed that if I did not, it was because she was already in a sound boat out on the sea, well away from what would soon happen.

Then I came up on the boat deck below the wheelhouse and I could see forward. The lights were still quite bright all over the ship and the orchestra was playing a waltz nearby and before me, at the bow, the forecastle deck already was awash. It was disappearing before my eyes. And now the people from steerage in rough blankets and flannel nightshirts and kersey caps were crowding up, and I felt bad for them. They'd been let down, too, trying to find a new life somewhere, and the gentlemen of the White Star Line were not prepared to save all these people.

A woman smelling of garlic pressed past me with a child swaddled against her chest and I looked forward again. The anchor crane was all that I could see of the forecastle. The blackness of the sea had smoothed away the bow of our ship, and I wanted to cry out the name of the woman I sought, and I realized that I did not even know it. We had never been introduced, of course. This woman and I had spoken together of life and death, and we had not even exchanged our names. That realization should have released me from my search, but in fact I grew quite intense now to find her.

There was a gunshot nearby and a voice cried out, "Women and children only. Be orderly." There was jostling behind me and voices rising, falling together in foreign words, full of panic now. I had already searched the first-class crowd in the midst of all that, and I slipped through a passage near the bridge and out onto the port side of the boat deck.

And there she was. There was order here, for the moment, women being helped into a boat by their husbands and by the ship's officers, though the movements were not refined now, there was a quick fumbling to them. But she was apart from all that. She was at the railing and looking forward. I came to her.

"Hello," I said.

She turned her face to me and at last I could see her beauty. She was caught full in the bridge lights now. I wished it were the moon again, but in the glare of the incandescent bulbs I could see the delicate thinness of her face, the great darkness of her eyes, made more beautiful, it seemed to me, by the faint traces of her age around them. She was younger than I, but she was no young girl; she was a woman with a life lived in ways that perhaps would have been very interesting to share, in some other place. Though I know now that in some other place I never would have had occasion or even the impulse—even the impulse, I say—to speak to her of anything, much less the events of her life or the events of my own life, pitiful as it was, though I think she would have liked India. As I float here in this strange place beneath this muffled light I think she would have liked to go out to India and turn that remarkable intuition of hers, the subtle responsiveness of her ear and her sight and even the bottoms of her feet, which told her the truth of our doom, she would have liked to turn all that sensitivity to the days and nights of India, the animal cries in the dark and the smell of the Bay of Bengal and the comfort of a bed shrouded in mosquito netting and the drifting to sleep.

Can this possibly be me speaking? What is this feeling? This speaking of a bed in the same breath with this woman? The shroud above me is moving in this place where I float. It strips away and there are the shadows of two figures there. But it's the figure beside me on the night I died that compels me. She stood there and she turned her face to me and I know now that she must have understood what it is to live in a body. She looked at me and I said, "You must go into a boat now."

"I was about to go below and wait," she said.

"Nonsense. You've known all along what's happening. You must go into the lifeboat."

"I don't know why."

"Because I ask you to." How inadequate that answer should have been, I realize now. But she looked into my face and those dark eyes searched me.

"You've dressed up," she said.

"To see you off," I said.

She smiled faintly and lifted her hand. I braced for her touch, breathless, but her hand stopped at my tie, adjusted it, and then fell once more.

"Please hurry." I tried to be firm but no more than whispered.

Nevertheless, she turned and I fell in beside her and we took a step together and another and another and we were before the lifeboat and a great flash of light lit us from above, a crackling fall of orange light, a distress flare, and she was beside me and she looked again into my eyes. My hands and arms were already dead, it seemed, they had already sunk deep beneath the sea, for they did not move. I turned and there was a man in uniform and I said, "Officer, please board this lady now."

He offered his hand to her and she took it and she moved into the end of the queue of women, and in a few moments she stepped into the boat. I shrank back into the darkness, terribly cold, feeling some terrible thing. One might expect it to be a fear of what was about to befall me, but one would be wrong. It was some other terrible thing that I did not try to think out. The winch began to turn and I stepped forward for one last look at her face, but the boat was gone. And my hands came up. They flailed before me and I didn't understand. I could not understand this at all.

So I went back to the smoking lounge, and the place was empty. I was very glad for that. I sat in the leather chair and I struck a match and I held it before my cigar and then I put it down. I could not smoke, and I didn't understand that either.

But above me there are two faces, pressed close, trying to see into this place where I float. I move. I shape these words. I know that they heard me when I cried out. When I felt the emptiness, even of this spiritual body. They were the ones who thrashed above me. Not swimming in the sea. Not drowning with me in the night the *Titanic* sank. I stood before her and my arms were dead, my hands could not move, but I know now what it is that brought me to a quiet grief all my corporeal life long. And I know now what it is that I've interrupted with my cry. These two above me were floating on the face of this sea and they were touching. They had known to raise their hands and touch each other.

At the end of the night I met her, I put my cigar down, and I waited, and soon the floor rose up and I fell against the wall and the chair was on top of me, and I don't remember the moment of the water, but it made no difference whatsoever. I was already dead. I'd long been dead.

"Woman Uses Glass Eye to Spy on Philandering Husband"

This is how I found out I could see things in another way: one night Roy and me had a big argument and this wasn't unusual for us, really, but he was calling me some pretty bad names and one thing and another happened and my glass eye popped out. He never hit me. Not like the husbands and wives I sit in front of to take down their words in the courtroom when they're on the stand. But Roy can talk pretty rough. So he says, "Loretta, you are one stupid bitch. Like right now. You should see the stupid look on your face. I've never seen a stupider face."

I don't know what to say about this. I'm real hurt, I know. But for a long moment there's just silence and there's nothing inside me. Like the silence in the court when my hands have been going a hundred and seventy words a minute and it's like they've been listening on their own and then they stop. Some woman is on the stand crying and keeping the sound down because it embarrasses her. I just sit and wait and I know she's crying but I don't even look up and I'm just empty. So I'm like that in front of Roy right after he says he's never seen a stupider face than mine, and he's waiting for me to tell him he's right, I guess, and then I hit myself. My hand just flies up and punches me in the face. It's the only logical thing, I guess. He won't quite do it, so it's up to me.

And all of a sudden I'm looking at Roy and he's a little alarmed, but in addition to his face in my head is another sight. A blur of miniblinds and china hutch and then the ceiling and the pink oriental rug and the ceiling and the rug and the ceiling. And then both of these things are in me, both real, both clear as can be: the temples on Roy's face throbbing and the little red light on the smoke detector flashing. My glass eye has flown out of my face and is lying on the rug about ten feet away and it's staring at the ceiling and I'm seeing through it.

Roy says, "This is too goddamn much, Loretta. You did that on purpose."

I close my eye—the one in my head—just to check this out and sure enough, I'm still looking at the ceiling. When I open my eye, Roy is gone. I hear his voice trailing out of the room. "Put your glass eye back in, Loretta. You disgust me."

I've come to accept this thing about me, having a glass eye. It's a very good one. A good match. So I'm not disgusted by this. I go over to where it's lying on the rug and I look

down. And I look up. At the same time. There's my cornflower blue eye lying there on the pink rug and all I can say
is that it looks astonished. Wide-eyed, I guess. And in my
head is my face staring down, one more cornflower blue eye,
and one sunken pucker waiting to be filled.

"Aren't you pretty," I say. And that's as big a surprise to
me as the punch.

That night Roy and I have made things up, as we always
do. We're lying in the bed and it's dark and I'm thinking
about all this. I've heard the lines before. From him. From
the stories of the women on the stand in divorce court. At
some point the men start getting angry over little things. And
they stop touching you. And then once you suspect them,
there's a brief time they try to be nice. Just for a little while. I
think these are the men who have some little bit of a decent
thing in them and they know that they loved this woman
once, this woman they're betraying. Roy gave me flowers
out of the blue a couple of weeks ago. "Why?" I say to him.

And he says, "Because, you know, because we're married.
And you're a good woman."

I've heard enough of other people's stories to know those
are scary words. I say, "That doesn't make sense, Roy. You
haven't given me flowers in . . . years." I almost say fourteen.
I know it's fourteen. But I don't want him to know I know.
It struck me once that a lot of time had gone by since the
last gesture like that and I figured out how much and then
I waited and counted. It's pretty sad, really, waiting those
years and noticing it all along and you don't even have it in
you to say something.

But I don't have to tell him the number in order for the mood to change in a big way. He gets real angry real fast. Another sign. "Then to hell with it," he says and he takes the flowers away from me and throws them across the room.

So I lie in the dark on the night my eye popped out and I could see through it, and I think about Roy and me. He's building an airplane in the garage. A real airplane, from a kit. He built one before and he flew it around for a couple of weeks and then he sold it. This is the work he has made for himself. The new plane sits out there and he goes to it every day and its bones are exposed, its ribs and its spine, and he puts his hands to it while I go off and take down the words of all the women who waited to speak and then it was too late to save whatever it was they had.

And that makes me think about what I have. I like Roy. This is Roy: he was a pilot when I met him, teaching people to fly Cessnas out at the airport. So on our first date he says, "I want to show you the greater Cedar Rapids area like you've never seen it." And he takes me up and we go a little way out of town and we do figure eights over the cornfields and we fly down low and we chase some steers across a pasture and we swoop up and ruffle the tops of some water oaks and we go and do a lazy ring-around at the grain elevator, and he's saying, Look at this, look at that, look what there is to see, Loretta. And he makes the Cessna leap and soar and he laughs and touches my hand to make sure I'm noticing all this. And what I'm seeing is this grown-up child of a man pedaling real fast on a trike and showing off for his girl, and I like that. I want to reach over and tousle his hair.

And he'll take me out to the garage sometimes and show me what he's done. Even still. Even a few days ago. Look Loretta. I'm putting her skin on.

But it's not the plane in the garage I'm jealous of. I wish it was just that. I think about how he still shows me sometimes what he's done and then I think of the woman he must be seeing and then I think again about him in that Cessna on our first date and he sees something off to his left and he lets out a little cry of delight and he doesn't say "Look" yet. Instead, he pulls us onto our side and we loop around and we're flying in the opposite direction and he's leaning over me and he says "There, Loretta," and I can see the sun in a thousand flakes on a little pond out in the middle of a pasture. "I'll always turn us around for you," he says to me and he means because of my eye. He took the news of my glass eye without a flinch even before he asked me on this date, and he even said it just made him realize how beautiful my other eye was.

But he can talk mean. And he can go to bed with some other woman. This is something I know from all the experience I've had with how these things go. And from the fact that he washed the sheets the other day without telling me. From our very own bed. This is a bad sign.

I'm thinking all this and I find my fingers moving faintly under the covers. Taking it all down. It's a familiar story to them. And then they stop. Because there's a silence in my head. And tears starting to come. I didn't tousle his hair when I first had the urge. I waited till the first time we made love, which was on our wedding night, which was the way I wanted it, which was still the way it was pretty much done in our circle in Cedar Rapids, even though it was the early seventies and everywhere else things were pretty loose. And on this night of my eye jumping out, I realize something about those ten or twelve months that I said, No. No, not till we're married, Roy. I realize that was the last time I really felt I had some control over my life. It was very nice, to tell the truth, those months with Roy before the marriage. Not that I didn't want to put my hands in his hair and all over him. But the holding on to my life was better.

Now I turn in the bed and he has his back to me and he's snoring softly and I reach out my hand to his head, but I don't quite touch him. His hair is the color of those galloping steers. And it's matted and swirled like them too. And I still want to take the tips of my fingers and furrow them through. Does she do that too? Now I want to furrow through like a plow. Like a sharp, hard plow blade. Somebody's been in this bed. Maybe this very day. I hold back a cry. I lie flat on my back and I look into the dark above me and I think of my glass eye watching the flash of red. My face burns like it should be setting off all the alarms. My eye. I know from countless cases that marriages can blow up on you from no more than this, some sheets in the washer and some suspicious kindness. I don't want to do it that way. And suddenly I have a plan.

The next night Roy is in the bathroom with the door closed. He's hiking his throat and passing wind in plaintive little moos—he has never passed wind in my presence in all the years we've been married, a thing I sometimes credit him for and sometimes blame him for. He either respects me or he has no sense of closeness to me. But I can hear him through the door of the master bathroom and I'm ready to act, but first, on an impulse, I pull back the quilt and look closely at the sheets. They haven't been washed. I bend to them and I sniff and sniff and I'm trying to catch a whiff of her perfume or her sex, but there's nothing but the second-day fade of Tide. Then the sounds end in the bathroom and I straighten and I've prepared a glass of water—a simple, clear drinking glass—and I pick it up and wait.

Roy comes out buttoned to the throat in his pajamas and ready for sleep, and he doesn't look at me right away. He goes to his side of the bed and he pulls back the quilt and he plumps the pillow. Then he realizes I'm not doing the same and he looks up. When I have his attention, though I make it seem I'm oblivious to him, I reach up and press and pluck and out comes my glass eye. I carefully launch it into the surface of the water, and though my face is turned away, Roy and the far side of the room ripple and then clarify and its like he's rising up but it's really my eye sinking and Roy rises, gaping, and then I've settled at the bottom of the glass and I'm looking at him from there, clear and steady.

"Loretta, what are you doing?"

"I called the doctor. He said to give my socket a little rest at night."

I don't like the way Roy shrugs, like he's saying it doesn't make any difference anyway. But that's what we've come to, Roy and me. So he climbs into bed and I carefully position my glass of water on the nightstand. I can see the whole bed from there. I've even put a vase of flowers on the stand, as well, to make the glass a little less conspicuous. He has not noticed the flowers.

Then the lights are out and we're lying side by side, and Roy hasn't turned his back to me yet. We're both lying with our faces up and our eyes are closed, and of course I'm seeing all of this. And I don't expect to be so moved by it, but I am. The covers are pulled up to our throats and our two faces float side by side in the dim light, drifting into unconsciousness together, Roy and me, with all we've been through, the flying around over Iowa, the living in a house. And even the fighting, getting all worked up together. There was even some sense of closeness about that. So there we lie, very quiet, in profile, only my good eye showing, and there's a land of sweet feeling in me about what I'm seeing, and a sudden sad feeling about what I'm doing. I almost fish my eye out of the glass of water and put it back in my head and keep it there. But I don't. I have to know. Things have popped out of their socket and I have to see.

The night was odd. I slept but I didn't sleep. I dreamed but I didn't dream. The only thing in my head, no matter how far deep I went in my sleep, was Roy and me lying beside each other, him putting his back to me pretty quick but turning to me again later in the night and even letting a sleeping arm fall around my quilted waist for a time, a gesture that seemed so natural that I wonder how many of these unconscious embraces there were that I never knew I got.

In the morning, I put my eye back in and I went to work and Roy went to his plane and, at some point, to this other woman. Or she came to him. But I wasn't quite ready to deal with that. I had to get Roy used to the eye in the glass. And so it went on like this for a week and then two, and one night I thought I smelled some cheap perfume in my bed and the next day I came home from work and found the sheets washed again, and then I knew it was time.

That night, while Roy was farting in private, I put the glass of water with my eye right in front of the flower vase and arranged the flowers to dangle down over the top of the glass. And in the morning I got up early and whispered to Roy that I had to get to the court to transcribe some notes and I put my sunglasses on and I went out, my glass eye still sitting on the night table.

It wasn't easy driving. I'm glad he just slept for a while or I might have killed myself on the highway. But it was hard enough just watching him turn on his back, his hair matted and cowlicked. He's still a handsome man. He draped a forearm over his eyes to block the morning sun coming through the cracks in the blinds. And he moved his legs and a horn blared at me and I was drifting into the next lane, drifting toward the movement of Roy's legs. I jerked the car back and looked in the rearview mirror and my face was there, masked by the blank stare of my sunglasses. I knew what was underneath, and the sunglasses wouldn't do in court.

So I stopped at a drugstore a block from the court building. There were some choices to cover my socket: white gauze stick-ons; flesh-colored stick-ons; a cloth patch with a band to go around the head, all in white with tiny pink flowers, like a baby's pajamas; a black eye-patch with a black strap, like from a pirate movie. But I was the audience, not the movie, and though Roy was still sleeping, he was getting restless, his head angled back now and his mouth wide open, his legs slowly swimming under the covers. Roy was the star of this movie and he was ready for his big scene. I grabbed a box of flesh-colored stick-ons and took them to the counter and a young woman was there, rather pretty but still struggling with pimples at her juiced up stage of life, and I wondered how old the woman was who would come before my waiting eye. This young?

I pulled out a twenty-dollar bill and I shoved it at this poor girl, ready to take out this fear on her, and Roy suddenly snaps awake. "What do you hear?" I say.

"Pardon me?" This from the clerk.

"Nothing," I say to her and Roy cocks his head. "Is it her?"

"Is it who?"

"What?" I say to the clerk. I don't know what she's talking about.

The girl shoots me a funny look and works fast at giving me the change and for a moment this seems suspicious. Like she's late to go see Roy or something. "You going off duty?" I ask her, even though I'm already letting go of this brief, crazy thought.

"No."

But then it's suddenly clear that the cock of Roy's head is him taking a crick out of his neck. He's moving lazy now. "Not yet," I say. "You bastard."

There's money being forced into my hand. "Count the change yourself. And you're an old bitch."

I'm moving away from the register and the girl says, "When I do get off, my boyfriend is here waiting." I'm out the door and Roy is sitting on the side of the bed wiggling his toes. Smug. He's watching his toes and he's feeling smug. I want to drive home right now and find something around the kitchen to hit him with. But at least I realize he isn't the kind to go hang around a drugstore to pick up a girl with pimples when she gets off work.

I'm in divorce court today and I go in to check my machine. Roy has been gone for a while, off in the bathroom, I think. I sit and load the paper and pull out the receiver in the back. We still use an old paper-punch machine and it makes this real soft, squishy sound under my hands. A nice sound. I roll out a few test words and all of a sudden Roy is there naked before me. He's still damp and it's been a long time since he just walked into a room with me while he was naked. Especially in the daylight. And even though it's just my eye and he doesn't even know it's there, I feel for a moment like he's doing this on purpose, just for me. Then something in me jumps the other way and I get hot: he's doing it for her, she's about to walk in. Then the juice goes out of me. I realize it's for neither of us. He looks around much too casually, and then he scratches his butt and heads for his underwear drawer.

I discover that my hands have been at work. I force my attention away from Roy and I pull up the folds of the steno scroll and I translate it back from the little runts of words I'm trained to put there. *He's naked,* I've written. *He's standing by the bed and it's been a long time since I've looked at that dangly part. You've got a sweet dangly part, old Roy. I wish you'd walk like that for me. But she's just out of sight. I can feel her. And this part is for her. Some woman knows this better than me now, you smug son of a bitch. Go put your boxers on, I don't give a damn about your body.*

This is a little scary for me. I tear off these words at the next fold and crumple them into my purse. I get up and I stagger down the hallway to our little clerk lounge, and by the time I get there Roy has thrown his clothes on and gone away. The bed is empty. The room is empty. I'm glad for that, and I pour a cup of coffee and I sit down in a Naugahyde chair. And I drink the coffee fast, so that it burns my mouth. I do that on purpose, I think. And then I think I should pour the coffee on my hands and burn them and it will give me an excuse to go home, and I should hurry there before anything can happen, maybe even before she arrives, and I'd come up the drive honking my horn, just in case she was early, and wait, pretending to fumble with my purse or something, waiting for her to slip, undiscovered, out the back door, and then I should go into the house and get my eye and put it back in my head so that I cannot see.

But I don't. It's enough for now that my mouth burns and the bed is empty. I convince myself that this is the way it will be all day long. He will touch only his airplane and I will return home this evening and things will go on just the same. That's what I want now, I think. Briefly.

They make the first call for court and I go out of the room and there's only this empty bed before me. I have not filled this bed either, I realize. I have climbed into this thing and lain, still and passionless, for years. The image of that floats in me with every step I take, every corner I turn in these corridors.

And then I am in my place before my machine and I am ready to think with my hands. There is a soft murmur of voices nearby, from the gallery, and we wait and the bailiff speaks and we all rise, and there is only sunlight creeping in my head. Thin stripes of sun from the blinds, moving slaunchwise across the bed, too slow to follow in the moment, but clear, also, in the longer minutes, like the hand on a clock moving.

I'm in a quicker place. My hands fly now. A woman is fed up. She wants out. She's sitting on the stand and she has a moon face and puffy eyes and she's near enough that I can almost reach out and touch her. There are children and she wants complete custody. Roy and me never had children and we never figured out why. By the time it occurred to us that this was so, we weren't caring anymore.

At the very moment that I think this, there's a pause for tears on the stand and I feel my hands write, *A sad story,* and it's about me, I think. Nobody's said those words in the courtroom. I tell my hands to pay attention. The bed before me is empty. The sun is gone from it. A tissue box passes from the judge to the woman and I'm writing, *You fly in figure eights over sunlight scattered on a pond and then you're lying on a bed in a dark room and you don't care to touch and you don't care that no life at all has come from you.*

I lift my hands and flex them, wring them together. Try to squeeze the distraction out of them. A nose brats softly nearby. Pay attention, I tell myself. I put my hands to the keys. The woman says that she's ready now.

And Roy and his woman stagger into my sight. They're in a clinch already and they spin across the room. I gasp. Aloud, I know. The judge has a round face too. It rises over the sidebar and I turn the gasp into a cough and hunch over the keys. My hands are afraid of the judge and they listen to the testimony, but the rest of me sees a woman not even thirty with a long, tangled hairdo like she went to bed wet and slept on her head. And she's got her arms around my husband and now her legs too and she and Roy fall on the bed.

I'm pressing this eye in my head shut. But it's my eye in the glass I'm wanting to close. I've seen enough. *He won't leave me alone,* my hands write, the words of the woman on the stand. But then, *They rip at each other's clothes. I will find the bed full of buttons tonight.* I open my eye and I can't hear the words in my hands now but I beg them to behave. "Please don't," I whisper, very low, and I'm talking to my hands and I'm talking to my husband and there is anger on the stand to drown me out and I whisper it again, "Don't. Don't."

And they are naked and she's got a butt that spreads more than mine and she's got something of a pot. "Flab," I whisper. But listen to me. Have I got a right to criticize? At least her flab is against Roy's and he wants it that way and she rises over him and he's on his back. And he's on my side of the bed. My side. "Move over," I say aloud.

"What's that?" the judge says.

"Can I hear that over?" I say.

The judge turns to the witness. "Please repeat your answer for the stenographer to record it."

Concentrate. I close my good eye again and I listen to my hands and they're saying something about a husband who won't listen, who doesn't care, and maybe I'm writing down this woman's testimony and maybe I'm just writing down the words in my own head. But I don't care either, to tell the truth. I stopped listening too, to tell the truth. The woman is thrashing her tangled hair around and her head is thrown back, her face lifted to the ceiling. I look at Roy. From the water glass beside our bed I look at my husband's face. His face will tell me.

"He doesn't care." I've said this aloud, I realize. Roy's face has told me at once. His mouth is set hard. His eyes are dead.

"Have you missed again?" the judge says.

"Yes, your honor. Is it, 'He doesn't care'?"

"You're right," the woman on the stand says, her face turning to me eagerly. The judge is a man. Her lawyer is a man. Her husband's lawyer is a man. She turns to me and she is glad to know someone understands. "You're right," she says.

The judge says to her, "We want to know what you said. Not if you agree with what the stenographer thinks she heard."

She's talking again, repeating, my hands are working. But then they stop. The woman in my bed has lowered her face and turns to look straight at me. Her eyes widen. Her mouth moves. Roy's face turns to me too.

And the judge says my name. He's looking at me too, half risen from his chair. "What's happening? Are you all right?"

The woman climbs off my husband and off the bed and she's coming to me, I realize. I rise up from my chair. As if I can confront her now, beat the crap out of her.

The judge says to the two lawyers, "Loretta is my very best stenographer."

The woman bends and her frizzy hair drapes down and she brings her face near to me, her nose bulging from the curve of my glass.

"What is it, Loretta? Your eye is bothering you?"

"Yes," I say and I'm glad I chose the stick-on patch that looks like a big Band-aid.

The woman has big eyes the color of dirty engine oil. I growl from looking at them and I put my hand over my eye, but it's only the patch.

"Can you continue?" the judge asks.

I think of Roy's dead face. He might put this woman aside. He might still want me. I say, "I don't know if I can continue."

"Do you want to try?"

"I don't know," I say.

But then the woman's hand appears out of nowhere and the water blurs and I can see only darkness and then I am eyeball to eyeball with this woman and then the room whirls around and falls over and I'm steady again, but looking sideways at Roy. His face isn't dead anymore. His mouth is hanging open and his eyes are wide in amazement and I realize that the woman has stuck my eye in her navel like a belly dancer's jewel.

"Oh no!" I shout.

"What is it?" the judge says.

My eye is approaching Roy's frozen face.

"My eye," I say.

Roy can't snap out of it and I think he knows I'm watching and I am very near him and his face begins slowly to sink. She is standing before him and pushing him down.

"Stop!" I shout.

"We'll get a replacement for you, Loretta," the judge says.

"No!" I cry.

"It's for your good," the judge says. "You're obviously in pain. You don't have to do this if you're in pain."

Roy pops back up and he and the judge are side by side in my head. Then Roy's face angles up and he smiles at her, a smile warm and full of shit.

"I'm in pain," I say.

"Then stop, Loretta," the judge says.

Roy's hand comes at me, snatches my eye, and I am flying into the bedclothes and darkness.

Now there's only the judge before me. My hand goes up and it touches the patch on my eye. Touches my face. Very gently. "I can leave," I say.

"Yes," he says.

And I do.

"Boy Born with Tattoo
of Elvis"

I carry him on my chest and it's a real tattoo and he was there
like that when I come out of Mama. That was the week after
he died, Elvis, and Mama made the mistake of letting folks
know about it and there was that one big newspaper story,
but she regretted it right away and she was happy that the
city papers didn't pick up on it. It was just as well for her
that most people didn't believe. She covered me up quick.
Not more than one or two of her boyfriends ever knew—
and there was many more than that come through in these
sixteen years. The couple of them who saw me without my
shirt and remarked on it thought she'd had it done to me,
and she never said nothing about it being there when I was
still inside her, and one of them got real jealous, as quite

a few of them finally do for one thing or another, this one
thinking that she was so much in love with Elvis that she had
him tattooed on her son and that meant she was probably
thinking about the King when the boyfriend and her was
thrashing around on her bed, and she never said nothing
to make him think that wasn't so and he hit her and I just
went out the door and off down the street to the river. We
live in Algiers, and I was maybe twelve then and I went and
sat on a fender pile by the water and watched New Orleans
across the way and I think I could hear music that time,
some Bourbon Street horn lifting out of the city and coming across the river, and it's the land of music I like to hear,
at times like that. There's other music in me but his. You
see, I'm not Elvis myself. I'm not him reincarnated as that
one newspaper tried to make you believe. I didn't come out
of my mama humming "Heartbreak Hotel," like they said.

The other boyfriend who knew about the tattoo didn't
get jealous and I laid there on the sofa bed that night and
from the next room I heard him moaning and laughing and
moaning and laughing and I knew Mama was regretting
his knowing and when they was done, this guy started singing some Elvis song, but I put the pillow around my head
and I hummed something else, "Saint James Infirmary" or
something like that.

And she almost never does this, but after they was finished in there, she come in to me. We have a shotgun house
with shutters that close us up tight and the only place I've
got is on the sofa bed in the living room, and the next room
through—the path that a shotgun blast would follow from

the front door to the back, which is how these houses got their name—the next room through was her bedroom and then there was the little hall with the bathroom and then the kitchen and the back door. One of her jealous boyfriends actually did fire through the house and the doors happened to be open, but it was a blunt-nose pistol and the bullet didn't make it all the way through the house, being as there was another boyfriend standing in one of the open doors along the way. Mama come in to me that night, too, cause I'd seen it all, I carried the smell of cordite around inside me for a week after.

So she come in to me after she'd done with this boyfriend who'd seen Elvis on my chest and she was smelling like the corner of some empty warehouse and I was laying there on my back and she come in and cooed a little and took me by the ears and fiddled with them like they was on crooked and she was straightening them and then her hands went down and smoothed flat the collar of my black T-shirt that I was sleeping in, but she couldn't undo what had been done. This guy had seen Elvis on me. She had tears in her eyes and I started wondering again if she was ashamed of me, if she thought I did something wrong, like I deliberately let this face of Elvis come upon me and that was a hurtful thing I did to her. But then she always said something that confused me about that. "How can you love a fool such as I?" she said to me that night.

It's a good question, I think. I think Elvis sold about two million records of a song by a name like that. But she meant it. And I didn't say anything to her. She waited for me to say oh Mama I love you I do. But she smelled like a stain on a riverfront wall and she never come in like this when things was normal and nobody'd seen me, and maybe she didn't know where my daddy was or maybe even who he was but he sure wasn't the guy in there right now and he wasn't going to be the next one either or the next and the few times I said anything about it, she told me she can't help falling in love.

But I didn't buy that. I couldn't. Still, I know what I'm supposed to feel for my mama: Elvis collapsed three times at the funeral for Gladys. But I'm not Elvis, and I'd stand real steady at a time like that, I think. Nothing could make me fall down. I would never fall down.

And this little scene after the second guy saw me was in that same year, when I was twelve. Now I'm sixteen. Just turned. And her birthday present for me was to bring home a new boyfriend from the bar where she works, a guy who looks like I'd imagine Colonel Parker to look. I never saw a photo of Parker, the man who took half of every dollar Elvis ever earned, but this guy with Mama had a jowly square face and hair the gray of the river on a day when a hurricane was fumbling toward us and he made no sounds in the night at all and this should have been a little better, some kind of little present after all. But Mama made sounds, and I'd gotten so used to them over the years I could always kind of ignore them and listen—if I chose to listen at all—to the men, how foolish they were, braying and wailing and whooping. At least Mama had them jumping through hoops: I could think that. At least Mama had them where she wanted them. But this new guy was silent and I hated him for that—he didn't like her enough, the goddamn fool—and I hated him for making me hear her again, the panting, like she was out of breath, panting that turned into a little moan and another and it was like a pulse, her moans, again and again, and I finally had sense enough to go out. But I'd heard too much already. Last night, it was.

But I don't care now. Tina come up to me in the hall this morning at the school and she said "I heard it was your birthday yesterday" and I said "It was" and she said "Why don't you ever talk with me, since I can't keep my eyes off you in class and you can see that very well" and I said "I don't talk real good" and she said "You don't have to" and I said "Are you lonesome tonight?" and she said "Yes" and then I told her to meet me at a certain empty warehouse on the river and we could talk and she said "I thought you weren't a good talker" and I said "I'm not" and she said "Okay." And now I have to think what I'm going to do about my chest.

Mama has worked hard to keep Elvis a secret. Mama even gets me a note from a preacher every year that it's against our religion to shower with other people. That keeps me hidden in phys. ed. at school. After that, it's pretty easy. Easy for me. Mama still has the one night a year when the note needs to be done up for the fall and she has to take the preacher into the next room. But I don't feel guilty about that. Not that one. It's like her putting her body between me and somebody who wants to touch me where they shouldn't. I don't mean the preacher. I mean anybody who'd look at my tattoo. That's how I feel it.

Because Elvis's skin is mine. His face is in the very center of my chest and it's turned a little to the left and angled down and his mouth is open in that heavy-lipped way of his, singing some sorrowful word, but his lips are not quite open as much as you'd think they should be in order to make that thick sound of his, and his hair is all black with the heavenly ink of the tattoo and a lock of it falls on his forehead and his lips are blushed and his cheeks are blushed and the twists of his ear are there and the line of his nose and chin and cheek, and his eyes are deep and dark, all these are done in the stain of a million invisible punctures, but all the rest, the broad forehead except for that lock of hair, his temples and his cheeks and chin, the flesh of him, is my flesh.

I want to touch Tina. She's very small and her face is as sharp and fine as the little lines in Elvis's ear and her hair is dark and thick and I want to lie beneath her and pull it around my face, and her eyes are a big surprise because they're blue, a dark, flat blue like I'd think suede would be if it was blue. I want to hold her and that makes my skin feel very strange, touchy, like if I put my hands on my chest I could wipe my skin right off. Tattoo and all. Not that I think that would happen. It's just the way my skin thinks about itself when I have Tina in my mind. And you'd think there'd be some big decision to make about this. But now that the time is here, it comes real easy. I will show her who I am tonight. I will show her my tattoo.

Mama used to tell me a story. When nobody was in the house and I was going to sleep, she'd come and sit beside me and she'd say do I want to hear a story and I'd say yes, because this was when I was a little kid, and she'd say, "Once upon a time there was a young woman who lived in an exotic faraway place where it was so hot in the summers that the walls in the houses would sweat. She wasn't no princess, no Cinderella either, but she knew that there was something special going to happen in her life. She was sweet and pure and the only boy who ever touched her was a great prince, a boy who would one day be the King, and he touched her only with his voice, his words would touch her and she could keep all her own secrets and know his too and nothing ever had to get messy. But then one night an evil spirit come in to her and made things real complicated and she knew that she was never going to be the same, except then a miracle happened. She gave birth to a child and he come into the world bearing the face of the prince who was now the King, the prince who had loved her with his words, and after that, no matter how bad things got, she could look at her son and see the part of her that once was."

This was the story Mama used to tell me and all I ever knew to do at the end was to say to her not to cry. But finally I stopped saying even that. I asked her once to tell me more of the story. "What happened to the boy?" I asked her and she looked at me like I was some sailor off a boat from a distant country and she didn't even know what language I was talking.

So tonight I go out of the house and around the back and in through the kitchen to get to the bathroom. She and the Colonel Parker guy are in the bedroom and I never go in there. Never. Before I step in to wash up I pause by her door and there's a rustling inside and some low talk and I give the door a heavy-lipped little sneer and a tree roach is poised on the door jamb near the knob and even he has sense enough to turn away and hustle off. So I click the bathroom door shut as soft as I can and I pull the cord overhead and the bulb pisses light down on me and I don't look at myself in the mirror but bend right to the basin and wash up for Tina and there's this fumbling around in my chest that's going on and finally I'm ready. I turn off the light and open the door and there's Mama just come out of her room and she jumps back and her sateen robe falls open and I lower my eyes right away and she says you scared me and I don't look at her or say nothing to her and Elvis might could sing about the shaking inside me but I for sure can't say anything about it and I push past her. "Honey?" she asks after me.

I slam the back door and I beat it down the street toward the river and it's August so it's still light out but the sun is softer this time of day and I'm glad for that. I start trying to concentrate on Tina waiting for me and I want the light and I want it to be soft and I keep thinking about how she says I don't have to talk and that makes me feel better and it makes me think that I'm right about Tina. And thinking that, I start to feel the eyes on me. I'm going along a street of shotguns that are like them twins you see in pictures that are joined at the hip and the stoops all have people sitting and catching the early-night sun and maybe a little breeze off the river and the men are smoking and the women are in their bare feet and they all are looking at me as I pass and they know the sight of me cause I been coming by here for a long time and they always say Hi.

So they know enough to see the difference in me. They know I got something on my mind now. They can see things like that. Most of them along here are black folks and Elvis had a special feel for them. They taught him his music. He always said that. And they know by just looking at me that I'm thinking about Tina. They smile at me and say, Evening, and I dip my head when they do because I don't want them to think I don't appreciate who they are but it makes me feel real funny this night because they're right. I'm thinking of the looks she says she's been giving me and I can see her eyes on me from across the classroom and they are flat blue and when they fix on me they don't move, they always wait for me to turn away, and I always do, and now I think maybe she's been seeing as much about me as these folks on the stoops. Maybe more. I think maybe when I show her who I am, she'll just say real low, but in wonder, "I knew it all along."

Then I'm past Pelican Liquors and the boarded up Piggly Wiggly and a bottle gang is shaping up for the evening on the next corner and they lift their paper bags to me and I just hurry on and I can see a containership slipping by at the far end of the street and I have to keep myself from running. I walk. I don't want to be sweating a lot when I get there. I just walk. But walking makes my mind turn. Mama's robe falls open and I look away as quick as I can but I see the center of her chest like you sometimes see the light after you turn it off, she comes out of her bedroom and her robe falls open

and I see the hollow of her chest, nothing more, and when
I turn away I can still see her chest and it's naked white and
I wonder why Elvis didn't appear there. She could've kept
her own secret then and known his too, and there wouldn't
never had to be nobody else involved in the whole thing.

I'm walking real slow now. I even stop. The ship has
passed and it looks like the street up ahead just runs off into
nothing. I can't see the river. But I know it's there and the
warehouse is not far now and I hear a sound nearby and I
leap a little inside and I turn and it ain't nothing but an old
hound up on its back legs trying to get into a trash can. I
watch him for a long time and he turns his head once, one
of his ears flopping over his nose, and then he goes on trying
to get in, though it doesn't look like he ever will.

And then I see that the light is starting to slip away and I
better get on, if I'm going to do this thing. And I turn down
the next street and I can see the river now and I follow it and
the warehouse has a chain link fence as high as my house
but it's cut in a few places and I find Tina on the other side
already and she sees me and she comes my way. She's wearing a stretchy top with ruffles around the shoulders and her
stomach's bare and she's in shorts and I haven't seen her legs
till now, not really, and they're nice, I know that, they're
longer than I figured, and we both have our fingers curled
through the fence links and we are nose to nose just about
and she says, "Get on in here."

I go in and she says "I was worried you wasn't coming"
and I find out I don't have anything to say to that and she
smiles like she's remembering that she told me I don't have

to talk good. But I can tell she's misunderstood that. I talk
okay in my head. I just can't let it out. She says, "I don't know
this place so well. Where should we go?"

I nod my head in the direction of the end of the warehouse, on the river side, and I feel a lock of my hair fall onto
my forehead and we move off and the ground is uneven,
rutted and grown over with witch grass and full of stones
and pipes and glass, and she brushes against me again and
again, keeping close, and I think to take her hand or put my
arm around her, but I don't. I want this to go slow. We walk
and she's saying how glad she is that I come, how she likes
me and how she is really on her own more or less in her life
and she has learned how to know who's okay and who isn't
and I'm okay.

And I still don't say anything and I couldn't even if I
wanted to because I'm shaking inside pretty bad and we
enter the warehouse through a door that says DANGER on
it and inside it's dark but you can feel the place on your face
and in your lungs, how big it is and how high, even though
you can't see real clear at this time of day, you just see the
run of gray windows down the river side and dust hanging
everywhere and there's that wet and rotted smell but Tina
says "Oh wow" and she presses against me and I let my arm
go around her waist and her arm comes around mine and
I take her into the manager's office. The light's still coming
in clear in the room and there are some old mattresses and
it doesn't smell too good but a couple of the windows are
punched open and it's mostly the river smell and the smell
of dust, which ain't too bad, and I let go of Tina and cross

to the window and I look at the water, just that. The river is empty at the moment and the last of the sun is scattered all over it and there's this scrabbling in me, like Elvis goes way deeper there than my skin and he's just woke up and is about to push himself out the center of my chest. I want to try to say something now. Not say. There's words that want to come but it feels like a song or something. I try to slow myself down so I can do this right.

Then I turn around to look at Tina and she must have gotten herself ready for this too because as soon as I'm facing her where she's standing in the slant of light, she strips off her top and her breasts are naked and I fall back a little against the window. It's too fast. I'm not ready, I think. But she seems to be waiting for me to do something, and then I think: she knows. It's time. So I drag my hand to the top button of my shirt and I undo it and then the next button and the next and I step aside a little, so the light will fall on me when I'm naked there and she circles so she can see me and then the last button is undone and I grasp the two sides and I can't hardly breathe and then I pull open my shirt.

Tina's eyes fall on the tattoo of Elvis and she gives it one quick look and she says "Oh cool" and then her eyes let go of me and she's looking for the zipper on her shorts, and whatever I'm thinking will happen, it's not that. It's not that. The secret of me is naked before her and I know she can't ever understand what it means, and then I know why Mama is naked so easy and why the face of Elvis didn't come upon her, why it come upon me instead, it was already lost to her,

and then I'm sliding away and the shirt is back on me before
I hit the warehouse door and I don't listen to the words that
follow me but I'm stumbling over the uneven ground, trying
to run, and I do run once I'm out the cut in the fence and
I hear a voice in my head as I run and it's my voice and it
surprises me but I listen and it says, "Once there was a boy
who was born with the face of a great king on his chest. The
boy lived in a dark cave and no one ever saw this face on him.
No one. And every night from deeper in the darkness of the
cave, far from the boy but clear to his ears, a woman moaned
and moaned and he did not understand what he was to do
about it. She touched him only with her voice. Sometimes
he thought this was the natural sound of the woman, the
breath of the life she wished to live. Sometimes he thought
she was in great pain. And he didn't know what to do. And
he didn't know that the image that was upon him, that was
part of his flesh, had a special power."

Then I slow down and everything is real calm inside me,
and I go up our stoop and in the front door and I go to the
door of Mama's bedroom and I throw it open hard and it
bangs and the jowly faced man jumps up from where he's
sitting in his underwear on Mama's bed. She straightens up
sharp where she's propped against the headboard, half hid by
the covers, and she's got a slip on and I'm grateful for that.
The man is standing there with his mouth gaping open and
Mama looks at me and she knows right off what's happened
and she says to the man, "You go on now." He looks at her
real dumb and she says it again, firm. "Go on. It's all over."
He starts picking up his clothes and Mama won't take her

eyes off mine and I don't turn away, I look at her too, and then the man is gone and the house is quiet.

It's just Mama and me and I have to lean against the door to keep from falling down.

"Woman Loses Cookie Bake-Off, Sets Self on Fire"

The day my husband died, I baked a batch of cookies. Hold-Me-Tight Chocolate Squares. Bar cookies that took forever to eat, never going away no matter how long you chewed, sticking between your teeth and up into your gums and making your hands quake and your tongue feel like it was about to dissolve. I put in two cups of sugar. That was a different time in my life. The end of a time, and the only way I knew to enjoy it was in the terms I'd lived it. So I put in two cups of sugar and three cups of milk chocolate chips and ate the whole pan-full that night. I was still shaking from it three days later at the funeral and everybody thought it was grief.

Even Eva. Of course, she wouldn't suspect it was anything else. Bless her heart. My friend Eva. She came up to

me by the open coffin and she was smelling of lavender.
She tried to make some lavender cookies once, its being
her favorite smell outside of the kitchen. Lavender is in the
mint family, after all, and I admire her now, thinking back,
for trying that. She couldn't possibly have had a real hope
that lavender cookies would please her family. Or maybe she
could. Still, her husband Wolf threw them across the room.
She blamed herself.

So at the coffin she said, "My poor Gertie. I'm so sorry."
And she took my hands, which were having this sugar fit
even then, and when she felt them, she rolled her eyes. "I
know how you feel."

Wolf had died almost a decade before. Barely turned
sixty. Arteries stuffed full of her Butterball Supremes, I suspect. Not that she wanted it that way. At the time, I wept
with her, thinking she was so dreadfully unlucky, thinking,
Oh God, how could I bear this myself. But when the moment came for me, when Karl went all white in the face
with my delft tureen in his hand at the dinner table and he
put it gently down before pitching forward into the Wiener
schnitzel, I began instantly to bear it, and my mind turned,
as it so often has in my life, to cookies.

Of course Eva thought she knew how I felt. I can't blame
her. We'd spent the better part of forty years thinking we
knew what each other felt. Most of my daughters were sitting
in the funeral parlor at that very moment with stricken faces,
and I figured I knew what they were feeling, though waiting
now before one of a hundred electric ovens in the Louisville
Fair and Exposition Center, waiting for our judgment at the

Great American Cookie Bake-Off, I'm not so sure. Maybe I don't know anything about anybody.

But Eva held my hand and she couldn't even recognize what was really going on in me. We'd quaked like that together over our kitchen tables more than once, laughing at what we'd just done, baked a batch of cookies and eaten them all. We could do that together, our little unconscious thumb to the nose. But we'd go right back and make another batch before Wolf and Karl and our children came home. These sweet little things were for them, after all. First and foremost for them.

So when Eva held my hand by the coffin, I looked into her face and I felt scared. Both for my having this dreadful feeling of relief—that's the only word I could find for what I was feeling about the death of the man I'd lived with for more than forty years—and for having this dear friend, my other self, so blind to what was really going on in me. I wanted to run away right then. Down the aisle of the funeral home and out into the street and home to my kitchen and I would bake more cookies—Peanut Butter Bouquets, those were the cookies in my head beside the coffin—I would make a batch of Peanut Butter Bouquets and I would eat them all and I wouldn't even hear the clock ticking over the sink or the afternoon breeze humming in the gutters or the daytime TV coming from the open windows next door and I wouldn't have to watch the laundry lifting on the line and snapping and falling and lifting again or the sun filling the empty lawn and then yielding to the shadow of our roof, sucked in by the shadow of our house like so much bright lint on the rug disappearing into the vacuum. Another sound. The vacuum. Roaring. And smelling like burnt rubber. My hands smelling of Lemon Joy. Or Lysol. Clean. Everything clean. Smelling clean. But all that was transformed by the turn my life had taken. I could bake cookies and sit and Karl would not be coming home that night and the girls were all in their own kitchens in various distant places and I would eat and eat and there would be no more batches to make unless I wanted to eat some more.

Eva expected me to be baking my Peanut Butter Bouquets in the Bake-Off today. Six months before Karl failed to finish his evening meal, she and I sat at her kitchen table and there was bright sun in the yard and sheets on the line—we neither of us liked the smell of the laundry when it came out of our electric dryers—and I could hear the sheets flapping. Eva and I sat at her kitchen table and there was a *Good Housekeeping* open between us and the full-page ad said that cookies were what made a house a home and now somebody was going to earn a hundred thousand dollars for baking her best cookies.

"Wouldn't it be something to win that?" Eva said.

"Yes," I said.

"Not that I need it. Wolf was so smart."

That was apparently true. Eva's life did not change in the slightest after he was gone. Like in the Bible the brother would marry the sister-in-law after she was widowed, Eva was married now to Wolf's interest-bearing accounts. Even though there was just his money, she kept her house the same way she always had, and she slept alone on those sheets that always smelled of the sun and the fresh air. And I always admired her for this. With a great swelling of the chest and a catch in the throat, I would speak of Eva's life to my other friends and my words would be full of admiration.

"You could do your Peanut Butter Bouquets," she said.

"You should enter alone, Eva," I said. "You win this year and I'll win next."

"It wouldn't be like we're competing," she said, putting her hand on mine in the center of her tabletop. "We'll root for each other. I want to do this with you."

So we sent in our recipes and on the same Tuesday afternoon, Eva and I got our letters. I was sitting at my kitchen table and I always worked my way down the pile of mail one thing at a time. So after seeing what Lillian Vernon and Harriet Carter had to offer, considering for about the hundredth time buying 20,000-hour lightbulbs, I found the notice from the contest sponsors. I read how they congratulated me warmly, Mrs. Gertrude Schmidt, and were looking forward to my joining ninety-nine other cookie bakers in Louisville in the fall and they said that my wonderful Peanut Butter Bouquet recipe qualified me, but if I wanted to invent something brand new, I could do any cookie I wanted at the final bake-off. Once they had their special one hundred, they liked surprises. You could use anything you wanted in your recipe as long as you greased your pan with their brand of no-stick aerosol cooking spray. Sincerely yours. Then the phone rang and it was Eva and she was weeping with excitement.

"I *will* do something new," she said.

"But I like your Butterball Supremes," I said. "They were Wolf's favorites."

She was silent for a long moment, and I was afraid I'd just made her sad, bringing up Wolf like that. I punched my forehead with the heel of my hand and waited out her silence. Then she said, thoughtfully, without any throb of pain, "Do you think it should be like a tribute?"

"No, no. I was wrong. Do something new. That'd be fun."

"You think so?"

"Sure," I said.

"Yes," she said. "I'll pretend he's alive and bake the cookie of his dreams."

At the time, this notion touched me. Now it makes me sick to my stomach. Eva was assigned the oven next to mine this morning and she's been baking for him, every moment. When we began, we all stood before our ovens, the auditorium so quiet I expected to hear sheets flapping somewhere, and our preparation tables were behind us and I glanced at Eva and her face was lowered and there was another face beyond hers and another and another stretching far away, all of us waiting to do our life's work, and I looked again at Eva and she was thinking about Wolf, I knew, and she was trying to ignore me, it had come to that, and I should have been ignoring her too, but there we were, and on the day we learned that we'd made the bake-off finals, my own husband was still very much alive. "Yes," I said to Eva. "I'm sure Wolf's spirit is still somewhere there in your kitchen. Make the cookie of his ghostly dreams."

I don't know what came over me to say that. I think I wanted to reassure her that he was still present in her life or something. But I said it badly, and she took this idea with a long moment of silence and then she said, "Yes." She said it with a throb of resolve in her voice and we hung up.

I sat for a while, thinking about breaking the news to Karl.

And it wasn't just the sounds of this place or all the minute things I saw every day of my life or the smell of my hands or my sheets or my upholstery that were mixing in my head and heating up and getting ready to pop out of the oven when eventually Karl pitched forward into his food. It was him too. It was him. It was me sitting there and not knowing how to say to him that there was actually a reason for me to go to Louisville, Kentucky, and try to do something. Damn my misguided Eva, I thought. It was a sweet "damn" that I spoke in my head, sweet and with an arm around her, but damn her for the whole idea, I thought. I shouldn't have to be facing this fact about my husband. I shouldn't have to be sitting at my kitchen table trying to figure out—with a quake in my hands that wasn't from too much sugar—how to talk to my husband about cookies that weren't for him. And I wasn't coming up with any answers.

As it turned out, I never did tell him. I put it off that night. He came home and he pecked a kiss into the empty air between us and he went to his recliner and he sat down and he opened his paper. Then there was dinner—pot roast and new potatoes and red cabbage and creamed corn and a tossed salad and Black Forest Honey Drops—a spicy little cookie that my grandmother taught me—and coffee, and there was no talk then either, not even a word about the cookies, though it had been some years since I'd made them and he ate them with obvious pleasure, dobbing the crumbs up with a wetted fingertip, and this was my test for the night. If he said nothing about these cookies, I would say nothing about Louisville. After the last crumb was gone and the last drop of coffee drunk, he leaned back and breathed deep and grunted the air out and said, "Good."

That didn't count. That was what he'd said every night for forty-odd years and he thought it counted, but it didn't count. Not that night. Not any night. Though I can feel this heat in me now—my cookies off to the judges and the hundred ovens growing cool and me standing here with the vast, steel-webbed ceiling of the auditorium soaring above me like in a cathedral—though I can feel heat now about Karl's monosyllabic approval, at the time I just let it go. I didn't get angry. I was off the hook for the night, after all. I wouldn't have to tell him about Louisville.

And the next night he was dead before the main course was through. And maybe he died from those cookies. Since they were from my grandmother, since they were from those days of my childhood in Germany—how far away they seem, but how clear—when my grandmother and my mother and I worked at a rough oak table with a coal oven heating nearby and the kitchen full of the smells of allspice and nutmeg and cinnamon and cloves and we made mounds and mounds of these cookies, maybe all the goodness that could come from the hands of three generations of women built up such a force of gustatory gratitude in the eater that if he did not vent it off with a lighting of the face and a warmth of the eyes and a tender loving touch and whole sentences of praise, the repression of that force would put a terrible strain on his heart and he would die within twenty-four hours. Maybe that's what happened.

I'd like to think so. He died, and when the ambulance had gone, I laid out the ingredients for the Hold-Me-Tights and even before I could grease my pan I knew what I was going to feel about my dead husband. I can't say I expected it, exactly, but it didn't surprise me either. I knew I couldn't talk about it. Anybody would take me for a hard, cruel person if they knew. Eva certainly would. It would shock her terribly. What did surprise me was what I began to feel about her.

She came to my house the next morning and rang the bell and I was still in the bed. I hadn't slept a wink. I'd lain catty-corner in the double bed, cutting across both spaces, and I'd thrashed around from the sugar rush, but it was more than that. The bed was empty. I lay on my back and scissored my legs and waved my arms like making angels in the snow and I couldn't get old show tunes out of my head and I hummed them in the dark and I moved my arms and legs in time. "Ol' Man River" and "You Cain't Win a Man with a Gun" and the one about the oldest established crap game in New York. It was a night filled with music and a kind of dance.

Then the sunlight came, and the doorbell. I peeked out my window at Eva. She had a plate of cookies. I figured I knew what they were. The fatal Butterballs. Sprinkled with powdered sugar. I had the same impulse myself the night before, but from Eva the sweetness of the cookies made me strangely restless and pouty and I let the curtain fall shut and I crawled back into bed and curled up and I didn't answer.

I did talk to her on the phone later in the day and I lied.

"Honey," Eva said, "I rang your bell over and over."

"I was asleep," I said. "I took some pills."

"I understand."

She didn't, of course. That's what I realized. I barely understood myself, at that moment.

"I brought you some cookies," she said.

"I'm sorry I missed them," I said.

"I put them in a Baggie and left them in your mailbox," she said.

"I'll get them," I said.

"I'm oh so sorry about Karl." She began to cry.

"Don't cry," I said, a little harshly, I think. But she didn't seem to notice.

"We're both bereft now," she said.

"I better get the cookies before the mailman thinks they're for him," I said and I hung up.

They weren't the Butterballs. I lifted them from the mailbox and they were red and round and fusing wetly together. She was experimenting. I opened the bag, and the smell—sweet and liquory—made my head spin. They were for Wolf. And Karl, not even buried yet, would have loved them too. I could see him licking the ooze off his fingers. I zipped the lock on the bag and carried the cookies through the house and punched the pedal of my stand-up galvanized trash can with my toe and the top popped open and the cookies were gone and the lid clanked shut.

I stepped into the middle of the kitchen floor and I found that I was breathing heavily. What was the rest of my life to be? That was the question of the moment. But I had no answers and I fought off the other question: what had all of my life been? I just stood panting in the middle of my kitchen and all I could hear was my breath. I couldn't hear the clock. The wind was moving the trees outside and no doubt was humming in the gutters but I couldn't hear that either. I could hear only my own breathing. In spite of the Hold-Me-Tights still coursing in my veins, I had to make some cookies.

Something basic. A simple chocolate chip. Chewy. I like them chewy. And I moved quickly to the cabinets and I laid it all out: uncooked oats, flour, baking powder, baking soda, salt, unsalted butter, eggs, vanilla, cinnamon, milk chocolate chips, granulated sugar, brown sugar. And the Crisco. I'd use a lot of Crisco. When I was a little girl I always wanted my cookies chewy and I never outgrew that.

And my own daughters were the same way. We'd make cookies in this very kitchen, always chewy, and I was lucky, I guess, that Karl liked them chewy, too, and on the first morning of my widowhood, I could see those girls around me in this place and the cookies were shaped into balls and they were on the cookie sheet and I said, "Come, my sweet ones, come and make your thumbprints here on the cookies," and they did, they came and pressed their thumbs into the cookies and these little images of my daughters went into the oven.

I was breathing hard again. So I made the chocolate chips, just the way I knew to do it. Two and a half cups of the oats. One and three-quarters cups of the flour. One cup of the granulated sugar. One cup of the brown sugar. And so forth. Going straight to the oven with the mixture—no chilling in the fridge—so that they would be chewy. And when they came out, I put them on the table and I could smell the sugar in them and my hands suddenly wouldn't hold still and the thought of the milk chocolate made my teeth hurt. So I let them sit. I did not eat even one of them.

But those were the cookies I turned to today. The Grand Chef and his entourage came down the row of ovens and we were all standing there in our oversized paper aprons with the Great American Cookie Bake-Off emblazoned on them and the TV cameras were following along and he had his clipboard and he asked each contestant what they were going to bake this fine day and the lady on one side of me said "Macadamia Mud Drops" and he wrote it down and then they all came to me and I could feel Eva's eyes on me from the other side and she was expecting to go up against my Peanut Butter Bouquets, but I said, "Chocolate Chip Cookies."

The Grand Chef's pen paused over the clipboard. He was expecting a more exotic name, I'm sure.

"With capital letters," I said.

"Yes," he said, with an understanding nod, though he didn't understand at all. I saw him print the name there all in capitals: CHOCOLATE CHIP COOKIES.

He moved on. I didn't care. I felt I could win. Somewhere in the auditorium there was a panel of tasters and the world for them was what the world had always been for those of us about to bake cookies in this place: mounds and rows and tin-fulls of sweet little lies.

After the funeral I sat in Eva's kitchen.

She was mixing cookie dough with a rubber spatula and she was weeping.

"I'm all right," I said to her.

She stopped and turned her face to me. "You've been very brave."

"I don't think so."

"Yes you have."

"It's not courage," I said. This was true as far as it went, but I didn't know how to say any more. Even for myself.

"Yes it is courage."

"It's crust," I said. "Worse. It's . . . I've been in the oven too long. All the sugar's crystallized, turned black, burnt up. There was too much of it to start."

"I don't understand what you're saying."

"I don't either," I said. "I've never burnt a cookie this bad in my life. Maybe the bottom blackened. Early on. When I was learning. But not this. What if you kept the oven on all day and night and then the next day and night and the cookies kept baking and burning and turning to a cinder. What happens to all the sweet things when they stay in the fire for years?"

"You're scaring me," Eva said, but when she said it, she didn't put down her bowl and come to me, she didn't come and give me a hug and tell me to go home and go to bed and take a cookie with me. She turned and began to stir her batter.

And I didn't have a clue about what was going on in me. Not a clue.

I didn't call her the next day, though it was my turn. Or the next. We didn't talk again. How did we know not to talk again after all those years of talk?

The Grand Chef passed on and a local TV reporter, a young woman who I bet never ate a cookie in her life except from a grocery store package, stuck her microphone in my face and the bright light came on and she said, "Why are you here?"

It was a good question, I guess. But there was only the one answer. "I've always made cookies," I said. "When you come down to it, people can't change what they've always done."

She and the microphone and the lights passed on, and I didn't look toward Eva, who was next. But I heard her voice, clear and loud, announce her cookies: Cherub Cheek Cherry Charms. The Grand Chef cried out in pleasure at the very idea of such a cookie and I bent over my hands lying on the top of my preparation table. My Great American paper apron crinkled. Some things can't change, but some things can. I'd brought the milk chocolate chips, but something had prompted me to bring semi-sweet, as well. Karl found them bitter, the semi-sweet chips. But Karl was also dead. He had another kind of bitter to deal with. I never much liked the semi-sweet chocolate either, but tastes change. Semi-sweet seemed right to me today.

And then we were all facing our stoves and the auditorium rang with the voice of the Grand Chef and he said,

"Bakers, start your ovens," and we did. And all the ingredients were before me and I laid them out, just as I had on the morning after Karl died. I sprayed my pan with their aerosol cooking oil and I mixed the oats and the flour and the cinnamon and the baking powder and the baking soda and the salt, and then I peeked at Eva. Her hands were scarlet. Whatever gave her cherubs' cheeks their blush was all over her hands. I stopped and watched her and I think there were tears in her eyes, and I guess they were for Wolf.

I turned to my cookies and it was time to make the sugar mixture. My hand went out to the granulated sugar, but I paused. My recipe asked for one cup of granulated sugar. But I'd had enough of that. I put in one cup of brown sugar. Just one cup of brown. The judges will thank me, I thought. After the Macadamia Mud and the Cherub Cheeks, they will turn away from all the desperate cloying and my cookies will touch them like something real, something true, like a mother's embrace. And they will chew and chew and the results will just have to wait because they won't want to stop chewing, and I will go home to my house tonight and I will make another batch of cookies just like this and I will chew all through the night and then on until the sun rises.

I lay in bed when I was a little girl and it was in the mountains, in Baden, and my mother and my grandmother both tucked me in and I'd secretly wrapped a cookie in the sleeve of my nightgown and surely they knew, the way they smiled at me and at each other, and it was Christmas or almost Christmas, that's how I remember it always, and it was no matter that my father was by the fire smoking and rocking and talking only to the other men, they did not even exist, there was no one in the world but these two women and me and there was the cookie wrapped in my sleeve that we three had just baked, and my mother and my grandmother pulled the covers over me and I wanted to grow up and be just like them, I would be large and warm and smart in the ways that women are smart, and under the covers, with the kisses of my mother and my grandmother still wet on my face, I ate my cookie and it was chewy and it lasted and lasted and it seemed that I would never even have to swallow, it would stay sweet in my mouth forever.

But of course I was wrong. Another life came upon me, and I know now that the cookie I had in my sleeve was good for the child but baked for the man by the fire, and if I go home tonight and make these very same cookies, the bed I will take them to is full of the smell of another man, even if he is dead. They are for him. They were always for him. This is what the two women I loved taught me. I have no doubt tried to teach my own daughters this same thing. I am nearly seventy years old.

And the winner has just been announced and Eva is weeping again, in joy. Her Cherub Cheeks have prevailed and I am happy for her. May she never wash her red hands clean. And now I have a match in my hand and I light it and my apron is made of paper and the cooking spray will grease my way home.

"Jealous Husband Returns in Form of Parrot"

I never can quite say as much as I know. I look at other parrots and I wonder if it's the same for them, if somebody is trapped in each of them paying some kind of price for living their life in a certain way. For instance, "Hello," I say, and I'm sitting on a perch in a pet store in Houston and what I'm really thinking is Holy shit. It's you. And what's happened is I'm looking at my wife.

"Hello," she says, and she comes over to me and I can't believe how beautiful she is. Those great brown eyes, almost as dark as the center of mine. And her nose—I don't remember her for her nose but its beauty is clear to me now. Her nose is a little too long, but it's redeemed by the faint hook to it.

She scratches the back of my neck.

Her touch makes my tail flare. I feel the stretch and rustle of me back there. I bend my head to her and she whispers, "Pretty bird."

For a moment I think she knows it's me. But she doesn't, of course. I say "Hello" again and I will eventually pick up "pretty bird." I can tell that as soon as she says it, but for now I can only give her another hello. Her fingertips move through my feathers and she seems to know about birds. She knows that to pet a bird you don't smooth his feathers down, you ruffle them.

But of course she did that in my human life, as well. It's all the same for her. Not that I was complaining, even to myself, at that moment in the pet shop when she found me like I presume she was supposed to. She said it again, "Pretty bird," and this brain that works like it does now could feel that tiny little voice of mine ready to shape itself around these sounds. But before I could get them out of my beak there was this guy at my wife's shoulder and all my feathers went slick flat like to make me small enough not to be seen and I backed away. The pupils of my eyes pinned and dilated and pinned again.

He circled around her. A guy that looked like a meat packer, big in the chest and thick with hair, the kind of guy that I always sensed her eyes moving to when I was alive. I had a bare chest and I'd look for little black hairs on the sheets when I'd come home on a day with the whiff of somebody else in the air. She was still in the same goddamn rut.

A "hello" wouldn't do and I'd recently learned "good night" but it was the wrong suggestion altogether, so I said nothing and the guy circled her and he was looking at me with a smug little smile and I fluffed up all my feathers, made myself about twice as big, so big he'd see he couldn't mess with me. I waited for him to draw close enough for me to take off the tip of his finger.

But she intervened. Those nut-brown eyes were before me and she said, "I want him."

And that's how I ended up in my own house once again. She bought me a large black wrought-iron cage, very large, convinced by some young guy who clerked in the bird department and who took her aside and made his voice go much too soft when he was doing the selling job. The meat packer didn't like it. I didn't either. I'd missed a lot of chances to take a bite out of this clerk in my stay at the shop and I regretted that suddenly.

But I got my giant cage and I guess I'm happy enough about that. I can pace as much as I want. I can hang upside down. It's full of bird toys. That dangling thing over there with knots and strips of rawhide and a bell at the bottom needs a good thrashing a couple of times a day and I'm the bird to do it. I look at the very dangle of it and the thing is rough, the rawhide and the knotted rope, and I get this restlessness back in my tail, a burning thrashing feeling, and it's like all the times when I was sure there was a man naked with my wife. Then I go to this thing that feels so familiar and I bite and bite and it's very good.

I could have used the thing the last day I went out of this house as a man. I'd found the address of the new guy at my wife's office. He'd been there a month in the shipping department and three times she'd mentioned him. She didn't even have to work with him and three times I heard about him, just dropped into the conversation. "Oh," she'd say when a car commercial came on the television, "that car there is like the one the new man in shipping owns. Just like it." Hey, I'm not stupid. She said another thing about him and then another and right after the third one I locked myself in the bathroom because I couldn't rage about this anymore. I felt like a damn fool whenever I actually said anything about this kind of feeling and she looked at me like she could start hating me real easy and so I was working on saying nothing, even if it meant locking myself up. My goal was to hold my tongue about half the time. That would be a good start.

But this guy from shipping. I found out his name and his address and it was one of her typical Saturday afternoons of vague shopping. So I went to his house, and his car that was just like the commercial was outside. Nobody was around in the neighborhood and there was this big tree in the back of the house going up to a second floor window that was making funny little sounds. I went up. The shade was drawn but not quite all the way. I was holding on to a limb with arms and legs wrapped around it like it was her in those times when I could forget the others for a little while. But the crack in the shade was just out of view and I crawled on along till there was no limb left and I fell on my head. Thinking about that now, my wings flap and I feel myself lift up and it all seems so avoidable. Though I know I'm different now. I'm a bird.

Except I'm not. That's what's confusing. It's like those times when she would tell me she loved me and I actually believed her and maybe it was true and we clung to each other in bed and at times like that I was different. I was the man in her life. I was whole with her. Except even at that moment, holding her sweetly, there was this other creature inside me who knew a lot more about it and couldn't quite put all the evidence together to speak.

My cage sits in the den. My pool table is gone and the cage is sitting in that space and if I come all the way down to one end of my perch I can see through the door and down the back hallway to the master bedroom. When she keeps the bedroom door open I can see the space at the foot of the bed but not the bed itself. That I can sense to the left, just out of sight. I watch the men go in and I hear the sounds but I can't quite see. And they drive me crazy.

I flap my wings and I squawk and I fluff up and I slick down and I throw seed and I attack that dangly toy as if it was the guy's balls, but it does no good. It never did any good in the other life either, the thrashing around I did by myself. In that other life I'd have given anything to be standing in this den with her doing this thing with some other guy just down the hall and all I had to do was walk down there and turn the corner and she couldn't deny it anymore.

But now all I can do is try to let it go. I sidestep down to the opposite end of the cage and I look out the big sliding glass doors to the backyard. It's a pretty yard. There are great placid maple trees with good places to roost. There's a blue sky that plucks at the feathers on my chest. There are clouds. Other birds. Fly away. I could just fly away.

I tried once and I learned a lesson. She forgot and left the door to my cage open and I climbed beak and foot, beak and foot, along the bars and curled around to stretch sideways out the door and the vast scene of peace was there at the other end of the room. I flew.

And a pain flared through my head and I fell straight down and the room whirled around and the only good thing was she held me. She put her hands under my wings and lifted me and clutched me to her breast and I wish there hadn't been bees in my head at the time so I could have enjoyed that, but she put me back in the cage and wept awhile. That touched me, her tears. And I looked back to the wall of sky and trees. There was something invisible there between me and that dream of peace. I remembered, eventually, about glass, and I knew I'd been lucky, I knew that for the little fragile-boned skull I was doing all this thinking in, it meant death.

She wept that day but by the night she had another man. A guy with a thick Georgia truck-stop accent and pale white skin and an Adam's apple big as my seed ball. This guy has been around for a few weeks and he makes a whooping sound down the hallway, just out of my sight. At times like that I want to fly against the bars of the cage, but I don't. I have to remember how the world has changed.

She's single now, of course. Her husband, the man that I was, is dead to her. She does not understand all that is behind my "hello." I know many words, for a parrot. I am a yellow-nape Amazon, a handsome bird, I think, green with a splash of yellow at the back of my neck. I talk pretty well, but none of my words are adequate. I can't make her understand.

And what would I say if I could? I was jealous in life. I admit it. I would admit it to her. But it was because of my connection to her. I would explain that. When we held each other, I had no past at all, no present but her body, no future but to lie there and not let her go. I was an egg hatched beneath her crouching body, I entered as a chick into her wet sky of a body, and all that I wished was to sit on her shoulder and fluff my feathers and lay my head against her cheek, my neck exposed to her hand. And so the glances that I could see in her troubled me deeply, the movement of her eyes in public to other men, the laughs sent across a room, the tracking of her mind behind her blank eyes, pursuing images of others, her distraction even in our bed, the ghosts that were there of men who'd touched her, perhaps even that very day. I was not part of all those other men who were part of her. I didn't want to connect to all that. It was only her that I would fluff for but these others were there also and I couldn't put them aside. I sensed them inside her and so they were inside me. If I had the words, these are the things I would say.

But half an hour ago there was a moment that thrilled me. A word, a word we all knew in the pet shop, was just the right word after all. This guy with his cowboy belt buckle and rattlesnake boots and his pasty face and his twanging words of love trailed after my wife, through the den, past my cage, and I said, "Cracker." He even flipped his head back a little at this in surprise. He'd been called that before to his face, I realized. I said it again, "Cracker." But to him I was a bird and he let it pass. "Cracker," I said. "Hello, cracker." That was even better. They were out of sight through the hall doorway and I hustled along the perch and I caught a glimpse of them before they made the turn to the bed and I said, "Hello, cracker," and he shot me one last glance.

It made me hopeful. I eased away from that end of the cage, moved toward the scene of peace beyond the far wall. The sky is chalky blue today, blue like the brow of the blue-front Amazon who was on the perch next to me for about a week at the store. She was very sweet, but I watched her carefully for a day or two when she first came in. And it wasn't long before she nuzzled up to a cockatoo named Gordo and I knew she'd break my heart. But her color now in the sky is sweet, really. I left all those feelings behind me when my wife showed up. I am a faithful man, for all my suspicions. Too faithful, maybe. I am ready to give too much and maybe that's the problem.

The whooping began down the hall and I focused on a tree out there. A crow flapped down, his mouth open, his throat throbbing, though I could not hear his sound. I was feeling very odd. At least I'd made my point to the guy in the other room. "Pretty bird," I said, referring to myself. She called me "pretty bird" and I believed her and I told myself again, "Pretty bird."

But then something new happened, something very difficult for me. She appeared in the den naked. I have not seen her naked since I fell from the tree and had no wings to fly. She always had a certain tidiness in things. She was naked in the bedroom, clothed in the den. But now she appears from the hallway and I look at her and she is still slim and she is beautiful, I think—at least I clearly remember that as her husband I found her beautiful in this state. Now, though, she seems too naked. Plucked. I find that a sad thing. I am sorry for her and she goes by me and she disappears into the kitchen. I want to pluck some of my own feathers, the feathers from my chest, and give them to her. I love her more in that moment, seeing her terrible nakedness, than I ever have before.

And since I've had success in the last few minutes with words, when she comes back I am moved to speak. "Hello," I say, meaning, You are still connected to me, I still want only you. "Hello," I say again. Please listen to this tiny heart that beats fast at all times for you.

And she does indeed stop and she comes to me and bends to me. "Pretty bird," I say and I am saying, You are beautiful, my wife, and your beauty cries out for protection. "Pretty." I want to cover you with my own nakedness. "Bad bird," I say. If there are others in your life, even in your mind, then there is nothing I can do. "Bad." Your nakedness is touched from inside by the others. "Open," I say. How can we be whole together if you are not empty in the place that I am to fill?

She smiles at this and she opens the door to my cage. "Up," I say, meaning, Is there no place for me in this world where I can be free of this terrible sense of others?

She reaches in now and offers her hand and I climb onto it and I tremble and she says, "Poor baby."

"Poor baby," I say. You have yearned for wholeness too and somehow I failed you. I was not enough. "Bad bird," I say. I'm sorry.

And then the cracker comes around the corner. He wears only his rattlesnake boots. I take one look at his miserable, featherless body and shake my head. We keep our sexual parts hidden, we parrots, and this man is a pitiful sight. "Peanut," I say. I presume that my wife simply has not noticed. But that's foolish, of course. This is, in fact, what she wants. Not me. And she scrapes me off her hand onto the open cage door and she turns her naked back to me and embraces this man and they laugh and stagger in their embrace around the corner.

For a moment I still think I've been eloquent. What I've said only needs repeating for it to have its transforming effect. "Hello," I say. "Hello. Pretty bird. Pretty. Bad bird. Bad. Open. Up. Poor baby. Bad bird." And I am beginning to hear myself as I really sound to her. "Peanut." I can never say what is in my heart to her. Never.

I stand on my cage door now and my wings stir. I look at the corner to the hallway and down at the end the whooping has begun again. I can fly there and think of things to do about all this.

But I do not. I turn instead and I look at the trees moving just beyond the other end of the room. I look at the sky the color of the brow of a blue-front Amazon. A shadow of birds spanks across the lawn. And I spread my wings. I will fly now. Even though I know there is something between me and that place where I can be free of all these feelings, I will fly. I will throw myself there again and again. Pretty bird. Bad bird. Good night.

"Woman Struck by Car Turns into Nymphomaniac"

I work in publishing myself and so I'm not going to sue that newspaper you buy in the supermarkets. I simply don't believe in it, as a matter of principle. But I categorically deny that what has happened to me since the accident is I've turned into a nymphomaniac. If I'm supposed to be a nympho, then I want to know why nobody ever called JFK or Wilt Chamberlain or Warren Beatty a satyr. Or all the millions of guys we all rightly assume have the same impulses as these public figures but less appeal or opportunity. Are all these guys satyrs? Isn't that, in fact, exactly the way all their brains work, just like the way mine is supposed to now?

But I'm not angry at men. I want to touch them. This is a revelation to me, sure. This has been coming on me since a New York gypsy cab and I had a blind date in a crosswalk on Sixth Avenue, sure. But this is a different thing from what the people at the *Real World Weekly* would have you believe.

I saw their editor-in-chief on the *Inside Scoop* TV show last night. They were demanding that he sort out the real from the unreal. If a doomsday meteor were really hurtling toward the earth, they asked, why should the only astrophysicist who seems to know about it be unreachable at his supposed lab in Albania? And why would an Albanian be named Desi, anyway? At this the editor-in-chief turned to the camera and said that the reach of *I Love Lucy* has always been greatly underestimated. And then he smiled a little half smile, this editor-in-chief, and he is a man perhaps forty years old with a sharp white part in his soft, black-cat hair and the smile punched a dimple into his left cheek and my hand rose, wanting to place the tip of my forefinger into that indent. "It's real," he said, speaking of the meteor.

I don't believe it is. Who does? But if it were true, and the world were going to end tomorrow, the only thing I'd regret was not having understood earlier what I understand now. No. "Understand" is the wrong word. That suggests a rational thing. And it suggests that I know what's going on. It's neither. So why should the word offer itself up at all? Am I mad? No. Mad people talk to themselves. I've discovered a part of me that I *can't* talk to. Or even about. But that part seems to know something.

A few mornings ago, for example. I was in my office and I was reading a manuscript. A prominent woman Orientalist trying to write a popular history of strange Eastern customs in little two-page chapters with zippy, freak-show headings and lurid illustrations. At that particular moment I was reading about footbinding, the imperial Chinese society tightly binding the feet of girls to create on their adult women crippled, distorted stumps. And these bound feet, bizarrely misshapen, nearly useless for walking, were made very secret; they were always kept beautifully covered up in silks and jewels. And here the Orientalist paused to point out the control that footbinding gave the men over their women, and I leaned back in my chair and looked out my window at the silver rise of the Chrysler Building and I thought about that for a moment. True enough, I supposed. Human relations always come down to a struggle for power. As a woman in a red tailored suit shooting for a vice-presidential title and three places a year on *The New York Times* best-seller list, I should know that.

But as I turned back to the manuscript, a young man flashed past my half-open office door. I found myself on my feet and at the door and peeking down the hallway after him. He was an editorial assistant named William, a junior editor's gofer and slush-pile wader, a Harvard lit major starting at wages as low as a McDonald's grill man so he can get into my office and do what I do. I followed him. I'd noticed him that morning at his desk. He was wearing a button-down dress shirt and a flashy silk tie with the Windsor knot pulled open, and when he finally gets into my chair and his name is on my door he'll change to bow ties and suspenders and he'll hire his lit majors from Smith. And even knowing all this, I didn't feel for a second that what was happening as I followed him was about power.

I found him poised over the photocopy machine, the automatic feed stacked with papers. What this was about was this young man, tall and solid, and his sleeves were rolled up. This was about the impulse I suddenly saw in him to break away from whoever his stiff, rich dad was. The knot on his tie was opened enough to show his throat, and his sleeves were rolled up to his biceps, and I realized I'd been wrong about him coming someday to bow ties, and all of this insight I suddenly had was there in his bare forearms and in the hollow of his throat. I forced a little cough and he looked over his shoulder and smiled at me and he shuffled his feet and ducked his head slightly in deference, but what I felt wasn't coming from the position I was in, it wasn't power, it was what I knew about him and what I still didn't know. He was William, no other. And he had a secret self and part of that self was a sly little rebellion from things that he and I would agree were pretty foolish. *That's* why I wanted to run my hand through the golden hair on his forearm.

And does it have something to do with the accident? Obviously something. I was blind to all of this before, it's true. One day in spring I stepped into the crosswalk at Sixth Avenue and Eighth Street and perhaps I was distracted by the thought of the Jenny Jones show, wishing it was the Oprah show instead, but Oprah doesn't do the real sleazy subjects, bless her pure and, for the moment, top-rated heart. So when your author is a Manhattan psychologist with a practice in masturbation therapy and a book called *Touch Yourself, Cure Yourself,* you take what you can get. In this case she was to be the resident expert on an upcoming "I Have More Fun with Me Than with My Partner" segment.

I was thinking surely *somebody* watching that show can read and suddenly there was the cry of a horn and I saw a flash of yellow coming at me and I stopped and I started to turn away. Then there was a terrific thump on my butt and I was suddenly on my back, my legs spread, and every pore of my body was flared open with a heat that felt like it was coming from the center of me. Though it was probably coming from the engine that was beneath me. I was spread-eagled on the cab's hood and looking at the clouds above me and my butt hurt, I guess, but other than that I was feeling pretty good. I reached up and brushed the hair away from my face, taking up a long strand and sort of twirling it around my finger.

Then a man's face floated between me and the clouds and his eyes were from way beyond the clouds, it felt, as dark as the darkest night sky. "Oh, lady," he said with an accent from somewhere on the other side of what was once the Iron Curtain. "You dream something when you cross, yes? A thousand miles away?" I realized he was the driver of the cab. His voice was gentle. He should have been cursing at me for walking against the light and causing him this kind of trouble. But he was making excuses for me.

"Remember," I said, "one end of the Iron Curtain was in a trailer park and the other was in a nudist colony."

"Oh my," he said, thinking I was delirious.

Not at all. Not at all. I felt very clear inside. I knew what connections I was making. This Eastern European man with the beautiful eyes and the sweet impulse to make excuses for the woman who was causing him trouble: I saw him rising from a bath towel on the shore of the Adriatic Sea and he was naked.

"He doesn't have a medallion," a whiny man's voice said.

"Please, mister," dark eyes said, not angry even at this buttinsky. "I will do what's right."

"Is it true?" I asked him.

He turned his face to me again.

"What?"

"About what you are?"

"Yes," he said, his voice violining into a whisper. "I am gypsy."

"I think I'm all right," I said. "Take me somewhere."

Later, in a room at the Hotel Dixie, he kissed me gently all around the edge of the massive bruise from his grill. And he was naked. Though the roar around us was not the surf on the Adriatic but the traffic from Times Square, he was as gentle in his hands and in his maleness as he was in his excuse-making.

"What thing was it you dream today?" he asked after our bodies had pulled softly apart.

"That's not the question to ask," I said and I found myself sitting up and bending near and looking at that male part of him. I was a little surprised to find myself doing this. I had never really looked at a man there before, only by accident, only out of the corner of my eye, more or less unwillingly. Now I wanted to see this man, this Anatole, and it came from his interest in my dreams, his unexpected gentleness,

I knew. I had a sense of him in these unseeable things: like I see the shape of a violin and feel that it seems just right for the sweet and sad sounds it makes, I looked at this man's body to see his inner self. It was turning from a taut young man into a wrinkled old codger. Doddering now and incapable of response as it was, I grew tender for it, in a certain way, tender as if for a beloved father who doesn't recognize you anymore, wanting only the best for him, in somebody else's care.

"What am I to ask?" he said.

"What's that?"

"If I am not asking what you dream when my cab hit upon you."

I smiled at him. "Ask what I will dream from that moment on."

"And so? Yes?"

I realized that I could not shape an answer to that, though something in me knew what to expect.

Is this nymphomania? I think not. I went to my apartment that night and I wanted nothing to do with my boyfriend. He's a very good-looking man but he reviews books anonymously for a pre-publication newsletter and he's got execrable taste and he's working on a novel about the Trojan War because he learned Greek at Notre Dame and I think it was the *idea* of a man who looks like this that made me take up with him in my life before the accident. But I know him. We rent a car now and then and go to the Hamptons and whenever anybody makes the slightest mistake in their driving near him, he honks his horn furiously and curses them and when I walked into my apartment and he was lounging in his distressed Levi's and flannel shirt on my couch and he looked up at me with what I know he intended as a sexy smile, I clearly saw his angry self-righteousness as a driver sculpted into his square jaw and curling up in his chest hair from the open shirt. And I had not seen this ever before in his body. I kept taking that body to bed and I never really saw it till that day when I was hit by a cab. Is that a symptom of nymphomania?

To myself I'm sounding entirely convinced about this. But perhaps not. Perhaps I've asked that rhetorical question about nymphomania too many times now and you're thinking the lady protests too much. It is true that I've been to bed with quite a few men since that day in the spring. But each of them was naked with me as an individual. I insist that's true. I know the alternative.

I was in a bar in Chelsea a few weeks ago. I'd been to a reading at Barnes and Noble by one of my authors, a first novelist, and I didn't want to go home. The boyfriend was thrown out and starting to savage all my authors in his reviews and I hate to admit it, but that was a trade-off I could easily live with. But there was no one else in my apartment that night either. The bar was small and the neon beer names burned coldly in the smoky air and a man sat down on the stool next to me. He was handsome and the sly wobble of his head and his little pucker-smile said he knew it. If you've heard too much protest in me so far and suspect the tabloid story of being accurate, then you'd have to expect this man and I would get along just fine.

"Hello," he said.

"Hello," I said.

"I just came over here to tell you how good you're looking tonight," he said.

"You appreciate women, do you?" I made my voice behave. No sarcasm. A straight question.

"It's what I am," he said and he leaned nearer. "Ontologically, I appreciate women."

I kept my face composed and I said, "If that's true, I'll do whatever you want."

His eyes widened and his eyelids fluttered like a silent film heroine. "Well," he said. "Well. We're going to have some fun, darling."

"But you have to prove it first."

"What?"

"Tell me about the last woman you slept with."

He furrowed his brow. "I don't understand."

"Do you want to go to bed with me?" I was still sounding sweet, but it was a firm question.

"That's why I sat down beside you," he said.

"Good. Then prove your appreciation. Tell me when was the last time you made love to a woman."

"Okay," he said. "Whatever turns you on. Two nights ago."

"What does her most intimate sexual part look like?"

"Look like?"

"Tell me all the details of it." He hesitated and I put my hand on his and said with a voice slick as K-Y jelly, "It turns me on." This was a lie, but it was his language.

He set his mouth and narrowed his eyes and cocked his head in an effort to remember. "It was . . . you know, an opening." He stopped. I waited. There was no more.

"That's all you remember?"

"Sure. What else is there?"

"I said you had to prove this."

He was getting pissed. "They're all basically alike," he said. "Any guy'll tell you that."

"Sorry, stud," I said. "You flunked the test."

I turned away and he went off cursing, and the fact is I can tell you the contours, the textures, the sweet little blue tracings of veins on the secret part of each man I've touched since the spring and they are each as different as their voices, as their minds, as all the subtle intricacies of their personalities. And they are precious to me, in their variety. When I lay on the hood of that cab and looked at the clouds, I knew that this would be so.

And it wasn't new to me, somehow, though it was something I'd left behind long ago. When I was a little girl I would lie in the field on my grandfather's farm in Connecticut and I would look at the clouds and I would see the usual things, of course, castles and horses and swans. But there were also faces in the clouds. Boys. These were boys that would appear over me as I lay on my back feeling the sun on my legs and opening to the life that awaited me, all the years ahead. The faces of boys would come to me in the sky and for a while I took them to be premonitions of boys who would one day love me, visions of their faces with wonderful, delicate varieties of brows and jaws and noses. And I loved them all, and each one loved a different aspect of me. This boy with a great pug nose was clearly a sports hero. I could ride horses with him. That one was a delicate boy with a weak chin, a poet; we would lie beneath the water oaks along my grandfather's stream and he would read poems to me. Another one with a high forehead was a banker and he and I would sit at night beside a fire and do my arithmetic together—I loved arithmetic and I thought I would always have these little puzzles to do. There were so many boys. Somewhere along the way, all that dreaming was lost and I just stopped expecting anything, really, from my sexuality. But as a child, I didn't think that one day I would have to choose just one of these boys in the sky. There were too many parts to *me*, you see.

The mistake I made was to talk about the change in my life to my masturbation therapy author. She was a psychologist, after all. And it was just conversation at lunch before the taping of Jenny Jones. I guess there was an implicit criticism about what she was saying in her book. You close the loop with yourself and it's not going to lead to healing. I didn't say it that way to her, but what else could she conclude? She was sitting across from me and eating red snapper and really enjoying it and it occurred to me that I hadn't seen her left hand come up from beneath the table for a while and I could see her vision of things: all the women of the world dining with their hands under their linen napkins and that's all they would ever need. So it was a mistake to tell her.

Then yesterday I saw the tabloid headline as I stood in a checkout lane at Gristede's and I looked at the story. They'd changed my name but every other detail was mine, and I knew I'd been betrayed. I abandoned my grocery cart and called my author. "What have you done?" I demanded. "Isn't that privileged information or something?"

"No," she said. "I've only got a master's degree in psychology."

"Are you sleeping with the tabloid editor?"

There was only silence on the other end of the line.

"Hypocrite," I said.

Then when I saw him last night on the television and when my hand rose before the screen to touch him, I knew what was next. My butt burned for him.

The offices of *Real World Weekly* were in a recently gen-trified brownstone in the East Village and I showed up this morning in a silk shift and I'd combed my hair out long and put a rose behind my ear. "Who shall I say is here to see him?" his mouse of a secretary said.

"Tell him I'm the woman from this week's front page."

She narrowed her eyes at me.

"Tell him I saw him on TV and I hear a taxi's horn blaring in my ears and only he can make it stop."

She gulped at this and turned her back to me and spoke low into the intercom.

He was there moments later, out of breath. He took one look at me and shot me that half smile with the dimple and he led me to his office at the back of the first floor. The room was stacked with newspapers and the clippings were all over his desk, and holding down a pile was a grapefruit-sized rock—dark and pocked—and on another pile was a brass stand with what looked like a shrunken head hanging on it. The little guy actually struck me as pretty cute.

"It's real," he said.

"Who was he?"

"Some Amazonian. He can predict the future. We did a story."

"And the rock?"

"Piece of a meteor."

I looked at the editor, and his sea gray eyes were intent on me.

"Like the one hurtling toward the earth?" I asked.

He smiled and the dimple appeared.

"Don't move," I said. "Keep the smile."

But he said, "Coming to kill us all," and the dimple went away.

"The smile."

He looked at me closely. "Are you really her?"

"I edited *Touch Yourself, Cure Yourself.*"

"Holy shit."

"The smile," I said.

"Are you here as outraged victim or as . . ." He hesitated.

"As nympho?"

"Ah . . . yes."

"Nympho."

That brought the smile back and I reached out and put the tip of my forefinger, just briefly, in that little spot. It was a sweet little soft place, this tuck in the face of a handsome man who was full of irony about the way our world was considering itself at the end of the millennium. That made me run hot for the secrets of his body. But his question was very interesting to me, really. That part of me born in the crosswalk was starting to blur the boundaries the editor was suggesting. Victim or nympho. Rage or lust.

After I drew my hand back, I said, "Men in the imperial Chinese court bound their women's feet. Did you know that?"

"I bet there are modern footbinders," he said with a rising in his voice like he'd just gotten a great new idea.

"Maybe so," I said.

"In Algeria, perhaps. Or right back in China. But that's a little remote."

"Would you like to understand them?" I said, and I was only just catching up, myself, with this turn in the conversation. I hadn't even realized the footbinders were on my mind, much less that I had some insight into them.

He snapped his fingers. "Appalachia," he said. "We'll look there."

"The men controlled their women this way," I said. "But they also created this intensely secret part on the women's bodies. The bound feet were supposed to be covered up always, but I think there were times, very rare, when, in the middle of the night, lit by candles, this secret of the body was shared." I'd moved closer to him and his gray eyes had turned back to me, though I sensed Appalachia lingering behind them. "They were like superpussies," I said.

Now I had his complete attention. "This is very interesting," he said, hoarsely.

"And that was the woman's control," I said. "I bet a man in imperial China would do anything the woman would ask just for the privilege of seeing this secret thing."

"I bet," he whispered.

"Do you find a woman's foot beautiful?" I drew my fingertips down his cheek.

"Yes," he said. "Sure." He was breathing heavily.

"Will you please start with mine?"

"Yes?"

"Please. As you know from reading your paper, I can't wait."

I took a step back and I slipped out of my shoes and I've got real good legs—I've had a lot of compliments in the past few months—and my feet are pretty, I keep my feet very nice. The editor-in-chief looked at them, and I could sense him trembling. Trembling and rising, in that secret part of him, a part which was hidden and bound until I chose to see it.

"Please," I said. "Start there." And I nodded to the floor, to my feet. "They've been covered up all day long. Nobody could see them."

He wanted to. I could tell. But he was hesitating. "Down," I said.

And he went down, onto his knees, and he bent to me and he began to kiss my toes and I thank my gypsy cab driver for teaching me how pleasurable all that can be and my hand was on the meteor and I picked it up and it was very heavy, very heavy indeed, and its heaviness sent a thrill through me, a sweet wet thrill, and I looked down at the straight white part in his hair, the very place where this meteor was about to strike, and I thought how sexy. How truly sexy is the secret shape of a man's brain.

"Nine-Year-Old Boy Is World's Youngest Hit Man"

This guy Ivan over at the Black Sea Social Club on Sixth and Avenue A says that when he went shopping as a little boy with his mama in Moscow he'd go to the one big department store in town and he'd stand in line and sometimes it'd be for hours and they didn't even know what it was they was waiting to buy. Then it'd turn out to be some shit like socks or suspenders or a rubber bowl. A Russian Tupperware party, he says, is four hours in a line with strangers to buy a rubber bowl. But they had so little, you just got what you could. That's why he does the things he does now in America, because it's the land of opportunity. And it's never too early to get in on the action, he says, cause you never had to wait to suffer in Russia. There are no children in Russia, he says.

I like it when Ivan tells me that. Up to this morning. When I'm feeling bad about myself, I say to him, I maybe ain't no child but I'm little, and he tells me it don't make no difference. It gives you an edge, he says to me. I know what he means, but I'm always thinking I want my hands to be bigger. I want that right now. I like the Makarov nine millimeter okay and most of Ivan's buddies at the social club use it, but it's just a pound and a half and not even six and a half inches long. Just right for me, but that pisses me off. Like being a Yankees fan. It's right there, up the subway line, but it's not what you really want. Besides, Ivan and those guys aren't real Americans yet, and I am, and the one thing I got off my long-gone daddy was his daddy's Colt .45 pistol. The Model 1911A1. They started making this baby way back in 1911, that's why they gave it that model number. And nobody's done any better. My daddy told me that. I stole it from him a long time ago, long before I did these things for Ivan. It was when my daddy was too drunk to see and I got lucky because the next day he walked out and my mama and me never heard from him again and he didn't even have his daddy's gun. I did. And it's like if Babe Ruth was still playing for the Yankees today and he was in his prime. Because this 1911 can still hit. I just can't quite hold it yet to do the job. My goddamn hands aren't big enough.

Last night I was sitting at our kitchen table and Mama was fussing around making it look like warming up Spaghetti Os was about a ten-step gourmet thing. She was still in her terry cloth dressing gown, my mama. She hasn't got a man hanging around her these days. Hasn't had for a while. And I was just looking at my little hands lying there on the table.

"Wally," she says to me. "Why you're always sitting around the kitchen in your undershirt."

"I'm waiting for you to give me a beer," I say.

She waves the can opener she's been struggling with for five minutes. "What are you saying? I never gave you no beer."

"I can wait."

"You're a little boy," she says.

"Mama, you don't know nothing about it."

She goes a little crazy at this, since we've had this conversation a few times before and she thinks she knows something about me. "I got eyes," she says. "I know you. I been around you for only nine years and at the start of that you was about twenty inches long. You don't think I know what a little boy looks like?"

So now she's got me looking at my hands, like two goddamn little bath toys sitting on the table, and I'm getting some feelings I don't want to think about. "Shut up now, Mama," I say.

She does. I should like that, but I don't, exactly. Then she says, real low, "So what will happen if I don't shut up?"

I don't have an answer for that. It's a stupid question.

She says, "Where do you go, Wally? When you're supposed to be in school. When you go out at night. I can't watch you all the time. What is it you're doing?"

I look at her and she kind of backs up a little bit, the can opener wobbling around in the air in front of her. I say, "Don't talk crazy. You're my mama." My voice—I can hear it like it belongs to somebody else—is as tiny as my hands, a piping cute-ass little voice.

"What kind of answer is that?" she asks me.

"What are you talking about?" My head is full of static now, like a radio that's off the station.

So I do both of us a favor. I get up and go out. There's a couple of guys jittering around at the corner and I know they just see me as some kid they can cut up easy and I left my heat back in my room, so I go the other way. And I walk around thinking about my dad. He was a big talker. He was always saying, I'm going to make this score, I'm going to make that score. I didn't know what he was talking about back then. I was just a lad. Four or five. Something like that. I was still playing on the raggedy-ass swings and shit at Tompkins Square Park. I'd swing up and down and the chains would scream like I was killing them and when I was way up high all I could see, all around, was funky homeless people living in cardboard boxes or sleeping under newspapers on the benches, guys that would grab at you when you went by, some of them, guys that would do anything to a little kid. Those guys were everywhere in the place I was a kid, and so were the old Russian guys sitting around playing chess.

Is my daddy going to end up like that, wherever he is? Not like the Russians. He don't play no games, as far as I know. Like the homeless people. Is he going to end up living in a refrigerator box with a stack of old Sunday *Times*? I don't know. All I know is I got his gun. And I figure he was full of shit about all the big stuff he was going to do. To tell the truth, though, I'd like to meet up with him someday and see how he come out. I was thinking about that walking around last night. And I was getting pissed. I was thinking, I got a score to settle with him. I do. I wish I didn't. I wish it was simple, about him. But what am I going to do? I've learned how things have to be.

The first time Ivan sent me to do this thing for him, I was pretty nervous about it. Sure. That was almost a year ago. I've got a birthday next week. I'll be ten, if I live that long. When I just turned nine, Ivan called me in from the dark open door of the social club. I was just passing time in the neighborhood. Kicking a flat Coke can around, trying to make it stop on the sidewalk cracks. Telling other kids who passed by that I was going to kill them. Stuff like that. So this voice from the darkness says, "Hey, little man. Come on in to this place."

I know the streets, and these guys were pretty new, but I could figure out this social club. It wasn't a place of perverts. It was a place of business. So I go in. This is when I met Ivan. "You want beer, little man?" he says.

"No," I say to him, though I like it that he asks me. Now I would've said yes, but the first time he asked me, I was straight from punk stuff like kicking Coke cans and I wasn't ready to say yes.

"You know how to get to Brighton Beach on subway?" he says to me.

Thinking about it a little later that day, I liked that being the first question he had about me. Not do you think you can kill.

"I can find it," I say.

"That's good," he says. "You really want to kill somebody?"

This is when he shows me the Makarov. He calls it a "PM."

I love that pistol at first sight. I bad-mouth it sometimes, thinking about the 1911. But it's the first one I knew I could shoot.

I ask him, "What's that, 'PM'? You just use this at night?"

"You can use it at night," Ivan says. "But it is Pistol Makarov. You want to hold this thing and maybe use it for me and then you can buy yourself something nice? You can walk around outside there and know you are big man already?"

My head was spinning from this. I had plenty of worries out there in the street. The guys in the park. The crackheads waiting in your building, in the shadows somewhere to grab you and if you don't have money to give them, they'll cut off your balls and sell them to herbal medicine stores for some kind of remedy. Stuff like that. I could use something to get people to pass me by.

"You want me to go blow somebody away?" I ask.

"You look like you could do it," Ivan says. He's got a pale face and his cheeks are sunken in and he's real tall, taller than my dad. He's waiting for me to answer and he's not even about to smile. I look for that, for the bullshit, for the tease. But I can see he's straight.

"Yeah. Sure. I want to hold it," I say.

He gives it to me and it's cold and it feels heavy at first. No heavier than a can of whatever dinner is tonight from Mama, but it feels heavier because it's small. That's a good way to think about me. I'm small, but I'm heavy. Like those stars somebody was talking about on TV. One spoonful weighs as

much as everything in New York City. I held my PM and it
was heavy like that and so was I. Any man try to touch me in
some way I don't want, they couldn't even move me an inch.
And now I had a thing that would kill their goddamn ass.

So I said yes to Ivan and he said good and he showed me
how to use the PM and how to fieldstrip it and clean it, and it
was real simple, only four parts, and I got my hands around
it real good and I was hitting the target in the basement of
the social club every time and Ivan never once changed how
he talked to me, like I was no lad, and he gave me a beer
later on and I didn't like it the first time.

But maybe that's the way it is the first time you do anything. One day I took the subway to Brighton Beach and it
turns into an elevated train down there. I like that. You get
to see all along the beach and even down to Coney Island.
You can see the big Ferris wheel. I went on that once, but
it wasn't so hot. I think I remember my dad throwing me
up in the air when I was little. I've seen dads do that sometimes, like in the park and stuff, and the kids laugh and seem
to like it, but those dads aren't so messed up that you just
know, even if you're pretty little, that he's going to drop you
sometime. I think going up in the Ferris wheel felt that same
way, made me think of going up and coming down hard.

Anyway, I went to Brighton Beach that day and killed a
guy for Ivan. I found myself thinking about my dad on the
train and I touched my PM, which was in a little brown
paper bag. Like I was carrying my lunch to school or something. That morning Ivan sits me at a table by the front window, though it's still dark cause the window's painted green.

There's a hooded lamp hanging over the center of the table and Ivan is sweating from the lightbulb, and he says, "This is that day you will become real man."

"I'm a real man now," I say. "That's why you know I will go and do this thing. You have to be a real man already to waste a guy. Wasting the guy doesn't make you the man." I figure if I can think as clear as that in school, all those dumb-ass teachers would stop messing with me. But I just dry up when I'm there with all the little kids. Arguing with a Russian thug in his club, I can do that.

He listens to me careful and thinks a moment and then he smiles at me. "You are too smart already. You turn into good hit man and someday we make you honorary Russian and you go far with us."

"Thanks," I say. "What do I do?"

And Ivan tells me about another Russian gang, the Arbat Gang, that's been pushing Ivan around. Ivan just wants Manhattan. He doesn't want to get involved with Brooklyn. But these guys won't leave him alone. They want to kill him. They're bad guys, they do their business all wrong. "When we take money from businessman," he says, "we give him good vodka, make him feel nice and protected. If he does not want to do business, we can maybe talk loud to him, lean on him little bit. But he for sure doesn't want to do business with those bad gangs in Brooklyn. Those gangs will send their friends in Moscow and murder that businessman's father." Ivan pauses to see how bad I think this is.

I don't bat an eye.

"And they kill his mother."

I wrinkle my nose at this. That's pretty bad. I think of my mother in her terry cloth housecoat opening the door of the apartment and she's been trying to get a goddamn can of something open so she can eat lunch and some guys blow her away. That's pretty low. But I'm still keeping quiet.

"And all of his little kids. His little malchiki."

Being a kid can be pretty tough. Gangs like that make it worse. "Look," I say. "What the hell you think I've been shooting your paper targets in the basement for?"

So I find myself on Brighton Beach Avenue and it's stuffed full of cars and everybody has just learned how to use their horns, it sounds like, and with the el sparking and squeal- ing overhead and guys hustling around in your face pushing sunglasses or knit caps or some kind of heart medicine and all kinds of other shit, with all that noise and action, I start to get a little nervous about what I'm going to do. Ivan says where I'm going, it's nice and quiet. Maybe one other guy to take care of at this time of day. But I'm starting to wonder.

I go on down the street and I'm passing by shops like Vladimir's Unisex and the Shostakovich Music, Art, and Sport School and the Hello Gorgeous Beauty Salon and there's just too many people around, all of them tall or fat or both and I'm getting goddamn tired bumping into belt buckles and saggy tits and I'm keeping my head down but they brush up against you, too, and I don't like to be touched. It makes me a little crazy sometimes. And I'm starting to worry that I'm going to take out my PM and use it on the next guy who bumps into me. But just thinking about the Makarov makes me calm down a little.

Then I get to the Gogol Cafe and maybe all the shit in the street is good because I'm ready just to do this thing and get it over with and I'm blaming this gang guy not just for killing little kids in Moscow but for making me walk through this goddamn crowded street. So this is his place where Ivan says nobody dares to mess with him and they never have and it should be easy. I don't know about that. It's somewhere between breakfast and lunch and the place is dim and it shouldn't be open but Ivan says to push the door, so I push and I'm inside and it smells like stuff that Chef Boyardee never dreamed of in a million years. And there's nobody around. All of a sudden I'm alone and if you want the truth, that's what scares me. Not what I was about to do or what might happen after that. It's standing there and, like, right away all the bustle is gone and there's only a dark room and if something is spooky, it's that. Being where there might be just one somebody else and you can't even see him.

So I go upstairs and there's a big fat guy sitting at a table with a white cloth and this isn't the main man but I think I'm going to have to deal with him anyway before long, so when he says, "What you doing here, little kid?" I just reach into my bag and pull out the PM and he says, "Nice toy, malchishka," and I guess I was lucky that he was making it so easy. I put a little three-shot cluster in the center of his chest and he hardly moves, he just leans back like he's finished his meal and he's making room so he can brush the tomato sauce off his shirtfront. But he leans his head back and it's not tomato sauce. I put my hand down low and walk toward the back of the place. From some back room a guy comes out and he's got a big nose that's full of bumps and this is the guy I'm here for.

He just sees what he thinks is a little kid walking toward him. He doesn't see what's in my hand or think even for a second that I could be dangerous, that I could be somebody he can't mess with. "What's going on?" he asks, not to anybody, really, maybe the fat guy, but Bumpy Nose is looking around like he just woke up from a bad dream. I know that feeling. So I put my first shot right in the center of his forehead and he goes straight down.

The place is real quiet again. But I ain't scared about it now. I know there's nobody can suddenly appear out of nowhere and put his hands on me. There's nobody else alive here but me. Maybe some cooks or something, making all those smells. Maybe somebody else. But they're as good as not there now. I know I'm safe.

I go back to where the fat guy has shut his yap. I look at him for a second, and I think what if he's like Wile E. Coyote or something. What if he jumps up and comes after me again. But I don't watch that cartoon stuff anymore. I just pick up my lunch bag and put my PM inside and I go down the stairs and there's people coming out of the kitchen, but they don't know who it is they're looking at going out the door and they don't mess with me.

That was how all this hit man stuff started. I went down to the boardwalk for a little while after that. The ocean was dirty gray, the color of the streets in our neighborhood, no big deal at all. There were old women out there in a lot more clothes than they needed by the water and there were old men walking along the shore talking to themselves, thinking they were back in Russia, I guess. There's a lot of messed-up people around. All I was feeling right then was that they didn't make any difference to me. Nobody did.

Ivan says, "Good man," when I come back to him that first time. He's already got the word about what I did. "The PM is yours," he says. "Here's the money," he says, and he gives me two hundred dollars. It feels like a lot. "We talk again," he says. "Do more business."

"Okay," I say.

Then I go home and my mother is watching TV in her robe. I'm standing there with my Makarov in the brown paper bag. She doesn't ask about it. "Why don't you dress?" I ask.

"I'm going to take a nice hot bath soon," she says.

I want to give her some money, but I'm afraid she'll think I made it dealing drugs.

"You should dress," I say. "Take care of yourself."

She looks over at me and kind of smiles. "Well, don't you sound like the man of the house."

"No I don't," I say. "No I fucking don't."

I go on back to the little runt of a room where I've got a mattress and a door that closes and I'm real nervous all of a sudden, I feel like going to my Makarov—I don't know to do what, just shoot it, maybe out the window—and I realize I've got to watch out about that. I've got boxes of junk in the corner and deep in the bottom one, under stacks of comic books, I've got my dad's gun, and I dig down in there and put the PM next to it, and I guess it's him that's bothering me. The man-of-the-house shit.

I lie down on the afternoon of that first time and I think about the weasely bastard. He smiled at me sometimes and that was nice and I wonder what was behind it. Did he think I was his little man? I don't think so. I was always a little kid to him. Kids get dumped. And after your dad beats it, kids get whatever the man of the house—whoever he is this month—wants to dish out, kids get, you know, whatever some strung-out stranger wants to do, the guy who's doing all that stuff to your mama's body since she's got no real man of the house, those guys do whatever they want to do to her, and if there's a kid, he has to watch out too, and what's he going to do about anything a guy like that wants, a guy about six feet tall with tattoos and shit, with a knife and with hands that can juice an apple with one squeeze, guys like that, little kids can't do anything about that. Little boys can't blow somebody away if they need to.

Then there's that guy who's my dad. I laid there on that first afternoon, and I thought about him and me having a score to settle if I see him again. But he was here all the time, before he wasn't here ever again. He'd say get the hell to bed and I'd go to bed and I'd close that door even if it didn't have a lock and he'd sit out there in the other room, I guess, drinking till late, I guess, and then I guess he'd go in to my mama and they'd do all that stuff and he'd be snoring away the next morning. At night when he was tired of me being around, even if I was just trying to watch TV, I'd just go in my room and he'd be outside there somewhere drinking and touching my mama, who loved him, and then he'd be sleeping and he never messed with me, once I was by myself. That's okay. All that's something. If he didn't make any big scores that I ever knew about, he was still thinking about it. All the time. He might be somewhere now. It's just if I caught up with him somewhere and I had my PM with me, I'm afraid I could get pretty angry at him pretty fast. I was just a little kid back then. I didn't know nothing then about how things can work.

How things can work is, I go to Brighton Beach three more times for Ivan. That's how they can work. And after the first time you don't even think about it. Once on the boardwalk and nobody even guesses it was me. Once in a barber shop and this time a couple of people see me and they can't believe their eyes, I guess, and I'm glad they can see me, in a way. This is what a man can look like sometimes. Like me. And Ivan says it's no sweat that they see me. Nobody in Brighton Beach talks to the police. They grew up in a place where you never talk to the police. And once in a car parked under the el pretty late at night, guys waiting for somebody else, I guess, not a little kid. Nobody saw me, but like the first time, there was two guys. They just couldn't quite figure out what to do when I pull out my PM and after I wasted the first guy, I had plenty of time for the second, who was saying some shit about me being a little kid. So that was four jobs, six guys. I've got eight hundred dollars hid away. I haven't spent a penny of it. It'd be for my mama, except I don't know how to give it to her. She about killed me after that last hit, I got home so late. She worries about me.

Which brings me to this morning. I wake up and maybe I'm dreaming. I don't know. I dream sometimes, I think. I just can't ever remember. But I wake up this morning and something makes me get up from my bed and I go to the cardboard boxes and I dig out my daddy's pistol. One night when he was drunk and he wasn't thinking about all the big stuff he was going to do with his life, he fieldstripped this thing while I was there at his elbow. On the kitchen table. He was talking about his daddy, remembering him. Maybe I was dreaming about that.

"This is the tricky part with the 1911," he said, and his hands were shaking, and it was only the first step. He said, "My daddy told me he was a big hero in the war. He killed a hundred Germans with this gun. But he was a lying son of a bitch about everything else. So he was probably lying about that too." While he was talking, my daddy was working out the plug at the end of the barrel and his thumb kept slipping. Then all of sudden there was a twang and the recoil spring flew out of the pistol and across the kitchen and through the door and landed in my mother's lap and she jumped up screaming. One second she was sitting there in her robe watching TV and then she was waving her arms and leaping around the room. I started laughing but my daddy didn't crack a smile. He turned to me real slow and he said, "The tricky part is not to let the spring fly out. You pay attention."

I stopped laughing right away. He was teaching me. I leaned against him and we waited for Mama to calm down and then I went and got the spring and I put it in his hand.

Now this morning I'm holding the pistol and it feels heavy, a good pound heavier than the Makarov, and that's a lot if you want to hold a pistol steady to shoot straight. I hold it with two hands and I reach my fingers up and they curl around the trigger. Just barely, but it's okay. That surprises me, but I forget sometimes that I'm still growing. So I've got my fingers on the trigger and the pistol is wobbling around and I'm crying. That pisses me off a lot. My daddy's making me cry now and it's a good thing he's not walking in that door right now cause I know I'd blow his fucking brains out.

I scrunch up my shoulder and dry my eyes on it, never letting go of the 1911, and then I try to just settle down. I pull the pistol up in front of me and it's still a little loosey goosey, but my chest kind of goes up and down and I swallow hard and the tears have stopped and the stuff I'm feeling sort of goes away. I'm supposed to see Ivan this morning, and I think what the hell. I slide my one 1911 magazine into the pistol and put it in my paper bag.

Later, I'm ready to go out and I'm passing through the kitchen and there's my sorry-ass mama sitting at the table in her slip. It's hot and she's fanning herself with a magazine and I stop. She looks up at me and smiles.

"You don't always have to make your own lunch," she says nodding at my paper bag and her voice is real tiny and she's still staring at the bag.

"I don't ever see you in clothes," I say to her.

"I ain't got no nice clothes," she says. "There ain't no clothes stamps."

"How much you need to buy yourself a lot of nice clothes?" I ask her.

"Need?"

"How much money'd that cost?"

She looks down at her toes and laughs at this. "I got expensive tastes," she says.

"How much?"

"Ten thousand dollars would about do it," she says.

"Okay," I say and I go out.

I go into the Black Sea Social Club and Ivan's in the back of the place shooting pool with one of the other guys I never talk to. A third guy, Nick, is sitting drinking a beer at a table. When Ivan sees me coming to him, he puts his cue down and circles around the table.

"There's the man," he says.

"Ivan."

"You have your lunch bag. Good."

I lift the bag for him. It feels heavy. I think maybe I should go back home for the Makarov before I head to Brighton.

"I have good job for you," Ivan says and he eases his butt back onto the edge of the pool table. "Important job."

"Okay," I say.

"A man at oyster restaurant on Mulberry Street."

"Mulberry Street? That's not in Brooklyn."

Ivan stands up again, and he comes to me and my neck is cricked back as far as it'll go to look at his face. I ease a few steps away and he eases with me so I'm still looking way up. I don't like it. "This is not Russian gang," he says. "This is worse thing. Mafia. You're not afraid, are you?"

"Why you ask that?" I say. "Shit no."

"Good," he says. "The Mafia, they eat little kids in their restaurants."

Ivan hasn't talked like this to me since the first job. I guess he thinks he needs to start from scratch to get me to waste some Mafia don, but he's got that wrong and I'm beginning to get itchy.

"I'll do it," I say, and I step back from him and he lets me. My neck stops cricking and I'm feeling a little better.

"Good," Ivan says.

Then the guy behind him says, "You win respect down there, they make you boss of Bambino family."

Ivan looks over his shoulder at this guy and I think he's unhappy with him, but when Ivan turns his face back to me, he's smiling. I know what a bambino is. But I let it pass. Ivan's been okay to me.

"Look," I say, "I got no problem doing this. I want ten thousand dollars."

Ivan's head kind of snaps. Then he gets this thing in his voice. "This is a lot of money," he says. "You know how much money this is?" And his voice is all stretched and gooey.

"I know how much it is. I want that."

"I give you three hundred. That's fifty percent raise."

"Ten thousand or forget it," I say and I say it hard enough so that he knows I mean it.

Ivan's sunken cheeks suck in some more. "Listen now," he says. "I give you very good gun. I give you a lot of money for little kid."

I straighten up and cock my head. "Wait," I say to him.

"No, you wait for me," he says. "I am doing good things for you all the time. You are not appreciating me."

"Fuck you," I say.

Now his face pinches and he slits his eyes at me. "You can't talk like that to Ivan. You got nothing till Ivan does things for you. You got nobody in world but Ivan. I am father to you."

This makes sense. So I go into the brown bag and out comes the 1911 and it's in my two hands and my first shot shatters the light over the pool table. We all of us just stand for a second after that and it's real quiet. Then the guy behind Ivan goes into his coat and the 1911 is flopping around in front of me like a goddamn can opener but I see his hand move and I follow it and my next shot is in the center of this guy's chest and he flies back. Now Nick is standing and I take him out with one in the shoulder and he's looking there like he doesn't know whose body this is and the next one in his throat and he's down.

And I've still got Ivan. He's grabbing around at his chest, maybe to see if he's hit, maybe reaching for a gun, which he doesn't seem to have. He looks at me and he says something in Russian. Probably something about being my fucking father. I put the next shot way up there in the center of his forehead and he flies back and the place is very quiet again and my real daddy's gun is feeling like it doesn't weigh anything at all, it's just floating there in my hands like it's part of me.

That was a few hours ago. I'm sitting in Tompkins Square Park and off somewhere behind me I can hear the swing chains creaking and I know I'm going to have to make a few plans soon. Some things are tough the first time you do them and then you get used to them. Some things you only need to do once. I figure if I ever meet up with my daddy now, him and me could maybe just talk.

"Every Man She Kisses Dies"

Bring on the sports heroes and the U.S. senators and the middle management bosses and the bad-seed uncles and the boyfriends your mama brought home from the cheap bars for the night, bring them to me and let them put their hands on me and their lips on mine and I'll kill the sons of bitches, giving them what they want. I might as well. Because the men I love, the ones who come to me gentle and speak sweetly and take it slow and look me in the eyes and try their hardest to do it right, they all die, as it is. From the touch of my lips.

He's gone for the moment, into the bathroom. He's surely afraid. He's so gentle and he must be afraid. I haven't kissed him yet. The room is white. The sun is coming through the window and the glare from the walls blinds me. I have nowhere to look, it is so pure and so empty. I listen for him. He clears his throat. Even that sound from him, coming through the closed door, has a tiny trembling in it. He is afraid. So am I.

Did I catch this from somebody? In some unprotected moment of passion? It's possible. How do you protect yourself from passion? And if you can protect yourself, how can it be passion? Must passion be gone from this world forever? Is that what we have to expect from each other if you suddenly find a man looking you in the eyes and you're sure he's seeing you and you can see him, real clear, and he says here is my body, take it, from my love for you, and I say here is my own body, I give you the same. If you are to really love each other, do you have to want this thing made of rubber between your sweetest flesh and his? If you find a moment on this earth when there is passion and there is love, shouldn't this barrier between the two of you make you sadder than death?

It does me. And it made me that sad even before I knew my own curse was worse by far. I have nightmares—they seem like nightmares but maybe they're just visions of the right thing to do in a world like this. I am about to kiss a man and we both really feel something between us and I say, Wait a minute. I go into the drawer in the nightstand and I pull out a foil pack and I tear it open and it's wax lips, big red wax lips, and I put them on and I murmur okay out of the corner of my mouth and we kiss.

The thing is, I believe in God. I still do. My daddy was a preacher and he would talk about the lips of a strange woman dripping like a honeycomb and her mouth being smoother than oil but her end being bitter as wormwood and sharp as a two-edged sword. Her feet go down to death, he would say, and her steps take hold on hell. It was from Proverbs that he was quoting, and he quoted it about once a year in our church and I would always remember it. Later on, though, I would read farther in Proverbs and I would hear the voice of those bad women and they would talk to the men passing by and they would sound to me like they were simply full of yearning and love. I have decked my bed with coverings of tapestry, with carved works, with fine linen of Egypt, one of them says. I have perfumed my bed with myrrh, aloe, and cinnamon. Come, she says, let us take our fill of love until the morning: let us solace ourselves with love. The Bible says the house of this woman is the way to hell, but I've thought about her often. And about God. I want to ask Him: What's wrong with seeking solace with love?

I went on to disappoint my daddy till he wouldn't even talk with me when he was dying. But I went to the hospital anyway and he turned his face from me and I went out into the hall and I watched my mother bend to him and they kissed on the lips. He would kiss her on the lips at night in our house, all my childhood long. He would do that. I think I forgave him his ideas for a long time more than I should have because I would see him kiss my mother on the lips.

I did not become a woman like the ones in the book of Proverbs. They were prostitutes and all I did was love the men I wanted to love, even if sometimes I made some bad choices. He knew I kissed them and sought solace with them. He would quote these verses in his church and look at me when I was there and think of me when I wasn't, and there was no difference in his mind between what I did and what he believed was an abomination.

I went away to the city. The big city, Chicago. And I suppose I've received my answer from God. He's fixed it so that I kill with my kiss. Even a man, I must assume, like Philip. A good and sweet man like him. The wood floors shine between me and the door to the bathroom. One large room. Utterly empty. All white. The sunlight is white, too, and in the great splash of it on the floor, there is not a single scuff mark. We are barefoot. We are wearing white linen. I am sitting in the center of the floor on a white down cushion. I think Philip loves me, and we have not kissed. He knows about me.

I'm not entirely sure when this began. I think it was up in Wisconsin a couple of years ago. It was when Daddy was alive and I went up there with a man named John. A poet at heart. And on the first day in some lodge on some lake up there beyond Oshkosh we ran into a man and woman from Daddy's church. An hour later Daddy was on the phone.

"We haven't talked much in recent times," he said.

"I know," I said.

"I'm not going to quote scripture to you," he said.

"Good for you," I said. "'He that reproveth a scorner getteth to himself shame. And he that rebuketh a wicked man getteth himself a blot.'" That was Proverbs too.

I heard him squeak in rage on the other end. But still he didn't do what came so natural to him. I felt a sneaky little admiration for him at that. But he did pick up my words. "Do you see yourself as a scorner and a wicked man?" he asked.

"Not a wicked man."

"Person then," he said.

"No."

"I was afraid that was so."

"So why did you call?"

"Because I love you."

"You sure it's not because I'm embarrassing you in front of your friends?"

"It's not their souls I'm worried about," he said.

"Bye, Daddy," I said, though I didn't hang up the phone. Neither did he. He didn't say a word. For a long time we just sat there on the phone listening to each other breathe. He wasn't going to be the one to do this. So finally I did. I put the phone on the cradle as softly as I could.

That night I was with John. He took me in a rowboat out onto the lake and there was an enormous red moon coming up over the trees. God was mooning us on the lake. John was rapturous over it. He started quoting poems, one after another, until I said, "Quiet. Please." I said it very gently and he obeyed without a flicker of hurt on his face and I appreciated him for that. "I want to hear you breathe," I said. And he drew near and put his face close to mine and I listened to him. Perhaps we dozed, as well, because a long time passed, and when we were conscious, we did nothing but listen and drift. Then the moon was very high. It had shrunk above us but it had grown much more intense. It was full and silver and cold. He'd made no attempt to touch me, though we had rented one room with one bed. He was a patient man, and I was filled with longing to touch him. So I put my hands on his cheeks and drew him to me and kissed him.

He sighed deeply and began quoting Chinese poetry. Written by Li Po, he said, a man in love with the moonlight. Then John turned and the image of the moon was floating right beside us in the water and he said, "Li Po would kiss the moon from love." And John leaned out of the boat and bent his face toward the moon in the water and there was only the slightest roll of the boat and he was gone.

"John," I said and I leaned out and waited for him to come up, tossing the water out of his face and hair and laughing. But he never reappeared. Not even to flail around and go down again. Nothing. And I feared at once that I had done it.

That fear passed, of course. No one could be sure of such a thing from one incident. My father died soon after, going to his grave without acknowledging me again, though, to his credit, this dismissal of me was not compromised even to try to draw some judgment-of-God lesson for me about John's death. I was depressed for some months, though I mourned John's death much more intensely than my father's. That made me feel guilty and so it was nearly a year before I went out again.

With Frank. Frank was a big man, square jawed and blond, and I felt almost fragile next to him. That's a nice feeling for a woman who's always been a little too tall and big-boned for many men. Frank made me feel almost dainty and we both worked at the Merchandise Mart and one afternoon he said to me, "Let's take our summer-Friday half day together and go to Wrigley Field."

So we did. We got on the el and headed for Addison and the friendly confines, and we got pretty good seats on the third-base side. About six rows in. It was one of those Chicago days when the wind comes in off the lake and it feels like it blows all the humidity away and the flag was stiff out over the bleachers and the ivy on the outfield walls was quaking and my hair was thrashing around and the Cubs were even winning. Frank turned to me, on this first date, and he gave me a smile as white as the moon and before he could look back to the next pitch, I moved my face toward him and he was ready and we kissed and our lips had barely touched when there was a crack in the distance and then a crack very nearby and his lips lurched hard into mine and slid away.

They say the ball rebounded out past second base. Ryne Sandberg made a one-handed catch. Frank would have liked that. But he was dead.

There is enough of my daddy's sense of the world in me to understand after two in a row that something was happening here that was providential. Not that I didn't test it some more. Not that my own improvised half-theology didn't cling to the notion of a God who would look on the yearning of a woman and a man to touch and take solace—or even a woman and a woman—any two people who found themselves in the terror and isolation of this life they did not choose—I half imagined a God who would look on such creatures and pity them and love them and try very hard to

show Himself in those moments when the two people, whoever they were, were letting go of their own selfishness and
fears and faithlessness and trying to find a way to cling hard
and long and permanently to each other. And if they failed
at that, God would see just the yearning for it as worthy of
a gift of all the grace a God could give.

So I kissed another man I liked and wanted to love, a
man with a life already rich in things. I kissed him one late
afternoon in my place, kissed him and lay with him, and he
left my bed because he had to be somewhere else and he
had to hurry and I began to think it was okay, I was silly ever
to wonder about this, and ten minutes later my phone rang.
He was calling me on his cellular phone from his BMW
convertible and he said, "I had to call. I had to tell you that
I have many things in my life, but your kiss is very special."
And then, I figured out from the police reports, he went
around a bend on the Dan Ryan Expressway, perhaps with
his eyes drifting out to the east, over the lake, to a moon still
pale from the verging sun, and he ran right under a stalled
semitrailer.

And the bathroom door swings open and Philip steps out
and he stops and he is looking at me. His linen pants and his
linen collarless shirt hang loose on him and I sense his body
inside there, naked and soft, and my heart is pounding and
my lips feel tumescent, as if they have their own separate
yearning and they are filling for him. With what? A kind of
venom utterly new to this world? A plague from God? Or not
so grand as that, after all. A plague simply from some sick,
mutant monkey in some dark jungle in Africa. He kissed a

sleeping traveler on safari who kissed a flight attendant who kissed a businessman from Chicago who kissed his secretary at the Merchandise Mart who kissed a mail boy who kissed me a happy new year at an office party. Perhaps it is as blandly horrific as that. Or maybe I am the scourge of the Old Testament, a modern harlot who dares love a man on terms quite different from a bunch of desert dwellers three and a half millennia ago and eight thousand miles away and so is doomed herself and destined only to bring doom.

Philip says, "I love you."

He's not said this before. Still, though we've known each other only the briefest of times, I've sensed it. We met at the Merchandise Mart. He brought some product drawings to show at a fair and he was lost in the building and he stopped me and he asked for directions. We spoke and I never even looked at his drawings. I showed him the way and gave him my phone number, in spite of what I knew about myself. In spite of that. He looked me in the eyes, he looked at me and did not look away and I gave him my number, and when he called me, before anything else, I told him. I told him all that I knew about myself. So he came here and he was dressed in linen and he is standing now before me and his eyes are soft on me.

"Are you afraid?" I say.

"Yes."

I feel a lifting in me, a warm rushing feeling about him because he loves me and because he believes me, and though this makes him afraid, he is here. He has dressed in white for me and I have dressed in white in this new and empty place where I live. I want this to be pure. I want to sit here with him on the floor and I don't know what it is that we will do, but it will be in a place without tapestries and without carved work and without myrrh and aloe and cinnamon. The linen is all right. They wrapped the dead body of Jesus in linen. He was killed by a kiss and then they wrapped him in linen.

He believes me when I tell him about this curse. I did not fully believe it myself even after the phone went dead from the Dan Ryan. I promise that it was still partly my disbelief that made me stop on Dearborn at noon a few weeks later. I was passing a construction site, and a worker there in a T-shirt and a hard hat was calling out to all the women going by. "Oh man," he cries as I pass. "That's just enough for me. Give me a kiss, honey."

And I stopped and some part of me still couldn't believe. But it's true that part of me did. And that part was thoroughly pissed at this man. He sought not solace. He sought not love. He would use the signs of those yearnings in order to control and demean and cast away. And so I turned and I moved into this space of unlaid stone and churning cement mixers and he was sitting beneath a web of steel beams and a half-risen wall and I went to him and his eyes widened and he flinched, expecting a blow, but I took his face in my hands and kissed him on the mouth, a kiss full of wrath. And I turned and walked away and I had not reached the end of the block before I heard a creaking of steel and a crumbling of mortar and then a long roar of falling concrete and beams. There was no doubt left in my mind.

It is tempting now, to send Philip away and to accept this role. I have eyes to see and ears to hear. I know easily from the pages of the newspapers every day that there are men who do evil and would ask for my kiss and all that I would do is comply with their wishes. I have done this once and I could do it often again. I have kissed in anger and killed. But surely only the wicked can consciously do that, can turn this act of love into death. And what does that suggest about a God who has brought these things into the world? Not to kiss in anger but in tenderness, in the yearning for closeness and care, and from this to kill. Is that not more wicked still?

Philip sits down now in front of me. "I'm afraid too," I say.

"That you will hurt me?"

"Yes. That. And another thing."

"What is it?"

I see my father's face in me, rising above his pulpit. He was right. On earth, the father is the image of God.

"I hated my father," I say.

"That frightens you?"

"Not exactly."

"What, then?"

I say, "I'm afraid that God is as loveless as he was."

He says, "Your father was not God."

"God gave me this evil."

"No. Not him. Did any of the men you kissed know the risk?"

"None of them."

"I do."

"Yes."

Philip draws his face near to me. "Then kiss me," he says.

"I want to kiss you. I want to. I want to touch."

"I understand. Kiss me. I'm asking you."

"We can stay here afterwards," I say.

"Yes."

"Will we be safe?"

"We will," he says. "I'll fill the room with furniture. I am a carpenter."

Then I kiss him.

"Doomsday Meteor Is Coming"

So we settle in at this new place in Westwood called "Coffee, Beer and Irony" and it's a Saturday afternoon, there's practically a whole weekend left ahead of us. I'm thinking I could stay here the entire time. When you find a place with a TV over the bar and a lot of light and hazelnut coffee, which is my favorite, and beer the color of Evian, you can almost think that the world isn't so bad after all. And the place even has tables with umbrellas out in the back, away from all the traffic. The Zima Garden. And I've got forty-two hours before I have to put on my suit and tie and go out and tread water for a while. I say I "have to" do that, but I choose to. It's a choice I make. I'm in my Converse high-tops today and that's me, but I'm no slacker. Not that anybody is pushing me to be. Tolerance is the word. Even Janis doesn't get after me about the job. She understands, in a certain way. The thing that's happening between us on this otherwise-should-be-fine Saturday afternoon isn't about my job, exactly.

She's across the room at a table with Peggy Sue and Liza. I'm at the bar with Justin and Seth. I look over at her and she's beautiful, my Janis Joplin-Hendrix Jones. Razored tangerine hair and six rings in her face and the poutiest, softest lips in the world with one of the rings through the lower one. I'm just beginning to suspect that I'm going to lose her. But what I don't know is if that's a real big thing for me or not. And all the while I'm sitting here looking at her, I have no idea that the end of the world is on the way.

Though I'm about to learn. We have our Zimas, the three of us guys, and I lift mine and I'm looking out the front window through it, watching the passing cars swim in my beer like tropical fish, and Justin says, "The world will be okay when all the rivers and lakes look like Zima," and Seth says, "Who are we kidding?" This stops Justin and he nods his head. Like yes. He hadn't thought of that point.

"Kidding about what?" I say, a black Firebird convertible billowing through my drink like a manta ray.

"That the rivers will ever run full of crystal clear malt liquor," Seth says.

"Don't tell me it's so," I say. "Where did we lose our idealism?"

"I left it in my other genes," Justin says.

So we all clink our bottles and drink to whatever that was. Meanwhile, the bartender is flipping channels and cursing

because the UCLA game is blacked out. "They're just playing over at the goddamn Coliseum and we can't see it," he
says.

Then he's got the Saturday rerun of *Inside Scoop,* and
Justin says "Stop. There might be something on Madonna."
So the bartender leaves it and goes about his business and
my attention is drifting, back to Janis. I look over my shoulder and I catch her eyes sliding away from me and she leans
toward Peggy Sue and they talk low.

It's about my nipple, I figure. Well, *our* nipples, actually,
one of Janis's and one of mine. She wants me to get my left
nipple pierced, the one over my heart, and she wants to do
the same, and that would mean we were joined at the nipple,
or something. More than that, I guess, but I'm not sure
what I think about this particular gesture. I'm resisting it,
and this is what's happening between Janis and me to make
this Saturday go bad. It's kind of a big deal, somehow, the
question of our two nipples, until I turn my face back and
I look up at the TV.

There's a guy on who's the editor of a newspaper called
Real World Weekly. He's a forty-something, a Double-Us,
from the look of him, and he's got an air about him, like he's
from the CIA or somewhere and he knows things that other
people don't. I've seen his paper at the supermarkets and
we always go "Cool" around it and laugh that in-between
laugh, that sort-of-with-it, sort-of-against-it kind of laugh,
that I'm-going-to-take-this-as-real, I'm-going-to-stand-away-
from-this kind of laugh, and that always feels good, one of
those laughs, because it tucks you away in a sweet little quiet

nowhere. So Justin and Seth are starting up like that already, but for some reason, I'm seeing this guy like through a real clear glass of beer.

He says that a meteor about a mile and a half wide is on a collision course with the planet Earth and it will arrive in about a year, though the scientists are all keeping quiet about this so as not to start a panic, so it could be any minute, really, or perhaps not for two years or so, but not much more. But when it hits Earth it will be like a fifty-million-megaton bomb and, to make a long story short, it will end all life as we know it on this planet.

Yeah, right. This is how you find out. Looking for the UCLA game while everybody's drinking beer and it's on a regularly scheduled show, and on a *rerun,* even, and nobody's paying attention and CNN doesn't have the story and never will.

Justin says, "This can be a unifying thing, you know? Bring all the earth together."

And Seth says, "No. We'll all kill each other before it even gets here. Every store will be looted. The justice system breaks down if all the maximum sentences are two years."

Like they don't believe it. I hear them and I'm thinking I should be throwing in some comment like that, but for some reason I don't. I sit here and my face has gotten real hot real fast and everything is seizing up in my chest and there's still enough in me of the guy in the Converses to step back and think, Hey, this is pretty weird, but it keeps going on in my body just the same.

The *Inside Scoop* people are asking the editor some tough questions now, I think, though I'm not concentrating very much on that. I'm already feeling that thing out there, hearing a static in my head like it's the solar wind peeling off it, if meteors have solar wind. Then the editor is looking right at me, at everybody in this bar, and he says, "It's real," and I know it is.

Justin says, "These are the guys who found out about that talking waterbed in Encino."

"I heard about that," Seth says. "That's true."

"True you heard about it?" Justin asks, seeking a clarification that I'm having trouble taking an interest in at the moment.

"I have to take a leak," I say just to get away for a little while and I put my Zima down and drop off the stool and my legs are having trouble holding me up, though I haven't even finished one drink, I'm still sober. I wobble off toward the back of the place and I'm drawing near to Janis and she looks up from her two friends.

"Linus," she says to me, "you look awful."

I'm feeling awful, too, and I sink into the empty chair at the table, next to Janis, and I'm trying to find a way to say this without it being taken wrong.

"Janis," I say. "The world's going to end, probably sooner rather than later, but in two years max."

Peggy Sue says, "My dad says I got to move out of the house in two years or else. So this is good. I won't have to find an apartment."

"I'm serious," I say. "There's a meteor." I stop. There's a lot of reasons to doubt me.

Liza says, "I'm going skydiving with Justin next weekend."

I'm not sure if she's trying to say something relevant here, maybe something about facing death, or if she's just changing the subject.

I look at Janis and she's studying me. She has a row of wrinkles between her eyebrows and she's touching the ring in her lower lip with the point of her tongue, something she does when she's thinking. "I'm serious," I say, lowering my voice and leaning toward Janis, like this is just for her.

Peggy Sue says, "Linus, you just have to do this nipple-piercing thing, you and Janis, it is so cool and so romantic."

All of a sudden I am very aware indeed of my nipples. And my chest as a whole, in light of this mile-and-a-half-wide ball of rock. And the top of my head and the soles of my feet. Something is happening to me and I'm starting to pant.

"What is it?" Janis says, also low, also bending near. I'd like to take her by the arm and walk her away from this table, maybe out into the sun, then I think, No. No. Not outside. Get under the table, for Christ's sake. But I don't have the strength for any movement at all at the moment, so I just try to control my breath, like a cowboy trying to jump up into the saddle of a moving horse.

Somewhere nearby a crowd is cheering. It sounds like a big crowd, but the sound is small. I think, That's how the meteor must look to those scientists. A very big thing but it looks small. And what I'm hearing is a portable radio nearby tuned to the UCLA game. I imagine the crowd all suddenly looking up and they make a great collective gasp.

"Let's take a little walk," Janis says.

I try to stand up. It's okay. One hand braced on the table, then the back of the chair, and my legs are working for the moment. She touches my arm, on a bare place, near my wrist, and her hand is impossibly soft. We move off.

She says, "Is it that you can't see us together?"

"No. I'm seeing *everybody* breaking up," I say.

"You have nothing pierced," she says. "This would be such a sweet thing for me."

"Like a virgin," I say.

"Yes," she says. "You are." And she puts her arm around my waist. I feel her bones there, her ulna, or her radius, whichever, what the hell good was all that education anyway, I think, with no world left. And her fragile bones: how simply, how completely, Janis would disappear. And all of us. I stop. We are in the middle of tables. People are all around. My face grows hot again, quickly. This woman smiling. That man dabbing at his mouth with his napkin. What a sad gesture, trying to keep himself clean while his death rushes to him, very near. Any day, perhaps.

"You're crying," Janis says.

"I've got something in my eye," I say, and I draw away from her. Her arm slides off me, but something remains, a shadow of her. I stumble on, down a passage, past a pay phone, a woman talking there, whispering into the phone, a man on the other end, no doubt, and they think they will marry and have children but there will be no more children, never again. I push into the men's room and into a stall and I slip the bolt and I back up against the wall and then I turn and lean my head into the wedge of the corner.

I don't know all that much about death. My dad's mother died, but I was very little, maybe about four, and I don't really remember her. I don't even remember whatever talk there was about Nana going to heaven to be with God, though there must have been some of that. Yes I do remember something. I grew up in Seattle. My dad works at Boeing. I think I had a picture in my head of Nana flying off to heaven in a 747 made by my dad. Which shows you what a little kid knows. If you've earned heaven, you should do better than airline food on the way. And they still had smoking sections back then. And the idea of God depending on my dad to get His souls to Him: no wonder I'm so unprepared for this moment. And there aren't enough jets in the world for all of us. That's a thing that makes me push my head harder into this wall. No seats. No room. Sold out.

I'm still crying, I realize. I dig at my eyes with the heels of my hands. I try to think about the bright side. The budget deficit will disappear. The whole national debt will be forgiven. Discrimination will end. All the handguns will fall silent. You don't have to go out and burn up your days working at meaningless things. You don't have to slowly drip your days away trying to do nothing. And you and Madonna will share a very intense moment.

I'm not sure I'm doing better, but my eyes are dry. I pull my head out of the corner and it feels like my skull has been compressed. I cover my temples with my palms and I worry, for a moment, that I've caused permanent damage to my brain. But that's another worry that instantly loses its bite.

I go out of the restroom and the pay phone is idle, and I stop there for a moment. I think about who I should call, just in case this happens to be the last day in the life of planet Earth, if the meteor is slipping past the moon even now and due on Earth in four minutes. My mom and dad, for instance. But the last time we talked, we actually got through about a five-minute conversation without an argument, and that would be a nice way to end it. And I think of Janis. I suddenly want to be with her. Even if she won't believe me, I'll be beside her when the thing itself, grown white hot from its plunge through the atmosphere, appears in the sky and persuades everyone. I'll hold her. You knew, she'll say, and I'll just hold her closer. I hurry now.

But she's not there. The table where she was is empty. Justin and Seth are gone too. Suddenly, it feels like death. One moment you're here and the next you're not. The meteor will take everyone in the world, but right now it's Justin and Seth and Liza and Peggy Sue. And Janis. Their sudden absence makes my legs go weak again and I think about falling down. But then I hear my name.

I turn and Janis is standing in the door to the Zima Garden. She motions for me, and I move toward her, a little bit pissed, for some reason. I realize what it is about parents when their child wanders off and then is found and the parents are happy, but mad too. Here. Take this whack. I was afraid you'd been harmed. That whole funny thing.

I get to Janis and she has her head cocked a little to the left. All her rings are visible—the three in her right ear, the two in her right nostril and the one in her lip, off-center to

the right. She's a right-brain person, she always says. Emotional. Well, I've reached a point where I put on a suit and
tie five days a week, but I'm emotional too.

She says, "Is your eye okay?"

"Yes," I say.

"Good," she says, and right away she slides off again. "If
you do this thing," she says, "you can always know who you
are even under your dress shirt and suit coat." She taps me
on the left nipple, very lightly.

I snap a little bit. "Back off, Janis. I like my nipple the
way it is."

Her face clouds up and all the rings quake faintly. She
turns on her heel and moves off and I follow her. The sun
is bright in the garden. More radios are cheering here and
there. Our friends have lowered the umbrella at our table
and are leaning their heads back, catching rays. Janis plops
down and I stop and I look up into the sky, half expecting to
see the flame of entry beginning. But there is nothing. Not
even a wisp of cloud. So I sit and I reach out right away and
touch Janis's hand. "I'm sorry," I say. One irony I don't want
is for the meteor to hit while I'm cordial with my parents
and arguing with Janis.

But she turns her hand at once and takes mine. This gets
to me. Even more because of the meteor. She doesn't realize
what's happening and yet she's quick to make up with me.
And it was me who snapped at her.

I look around. Everybody's just going on with their business. I feel very tender for them as they drink their coffee
and their beer and they eat their croissants and they chat and

they read their newspapers (which have missed the biggest story in history). Then I turn to the four lifted chins and four sets of closed eyes in front of me and I look at Janis, her face turned a little away. We are still clutching each other's hands. I look at her rings. The one in her lip: I focus on that one. What is it I feel? The ring says she is soft, her flesh can part and yield to this tiny hard thing. It stirs me a little, too, that something is inside her. I want to be inside her. The ring carries me inside her body. And the ring says she is vulnerable. A thing can break through her, rip her open.

"You have to listen to me," I say. Loud enough for the four chins to sink and the eyes to open. Janis turns her face to me. "Something is happening," I say. They look at me blankly. The thing I have to say is too much *there*. It's just there. There's no angle on it. There's no in-between. No place to hide. But still I have to try. "I have something important to say."

Then we're in shadow. It comes quickly over us and I know there are no clouds and Justin's eyes go up first and he lifts his face and his mouth opens, in wonder, and then Seth is looking and Peggy Sue and Liza and the shadow is cold, very cold, and they're all filled with awe and, I think, with terror, but Janis isn't looking. She's looking at me.

She asks, very gently, "What do you have to say?"

I squeeze her hand and I draw near and I lean to her and I kiss that place where the ring slips through her lip, I kiss that tiny point of entry, a single clear pixel in the image of her mortality. I pull back and her eyes are sad, I think, and perhaps she has peeked overhead, perhaps she knows what it is I have to say. So I turn my head and it takes all my energy. I lift my eyes.

And overhead is the Goodyear blimp. I can hear the bratty little hum of its motors and the shadow of it tootles by and we are in the sun again and the blimp heads off back to the Coliseum and the marching bands.

Now we are all facing each other once more. What I know is still what I know. The doomsday meteor is coming, like the man said. But I find that it's not what I have to say to my friends.

"So, yes?" Justin asks. "What is it, Linus?"

I look at them one at a time, my friends, my fragile, doomed friends. And I look at Janis and she is waiting. I say, "I want you all to know that Janis and I are going to have our left nipples pierced. It will be a sign of something very important."

Janis's eyes fill quickly with tears and so do mine, and Peggy Sue says, "How romantic."

"Help Me Find My Spaceman Lover"

I never thought I could fall for a spaceman. I mean, you see them in the newspaper and they kind of give you the willies, all skinny and hairless and wiggly looking, and if you touched one, even to shake hands, you just know it would be like when you were about fifteen and you were with an Earth boy and you were sweet on him but there was this thing he wanted, and you finally said okay, but only rub-a-dub, which is what we called it around these parts when I was younger, and it was the first time ever that you touched . . . well, you know what I'm talking about. Anyway, that's what it's always seemed like to me with spacemen, and most everybody around here feels about the same way, I'm sure. Folks in Bovary, Alabama, and environs—by which I mean the KOA campground off the interstate and the new trailer park out past the quarry—everybody in Bovary is used to people being a certain way, to look at and to talk to and so forth. Take my daddy. When I showed him a few years ago in the newspaper how a spaceman had endorsed Bill Clinton for president and they had a picture of a spaceman standing there next to Bill Clinton—without any visible clothes on, by the way—the spaceman, that is, not Bill Clinton, though I wouldn't put it past him, to tell the truth, and I'm not surprised at anything they might do over in Little Rock. But I showed my daddy the newspaper and he took a look at the spaceman and he snorted and said that he wasn't surprised people like that was supporting the Democrats, people like that don't even look American, and I said no, Daddy, he's a spaceman, and he said people like that don't even look human, and I said no, Daddy, he's not human, and my daddy said, that's what I'm saying, make him get a job.

But I did fall for a spaceman, as it turned out, fell pretty hard. I met him in the parking lot at the twenty-four-hour Wal-Mart. We used to have a regular old Wal-Mart that would close at nine o'clock and when they turned it into a Super Center a lot of people in Bovary thought that no good would come of it, encouraging people to stay up all night. Americans go to bed early and get up early, my daddy said. But I have trouble sleeping sometimes. I live in the old trailer park out the state highway and it's not too far from the Wal-Mart and I live there with my yellow cat Eddie. I am forty years old and I was married once, to a telephone installer who fell in love with cable TV. There's no cable TV in Bovary yet, though with a twenty-four-hour Wal-Mart, it's probably not too far behind. It won't come soon enough to save my marriage, however. Not that I wanted it to. He told me he just *had* to install cable TV, telephones weren't fulfilling him, and he was going away for good to Mobile and he didn't want me to go with him, this was the end for us, and I was understanding the parts about it being the end but he was going on about fiber optics and things that I didn't really follow. So I said fine and he went away, and even if he'd wanted me to go with him, I wouldn't have done it. I've only been to Mobile a couple of times and I didn't take to it. Bovary is just right for me. At least that's what I thought when it had to do with my ex-husband, and that kind of thinking just stayed with me, like a grape-juice stain on your housedress, and I am full of regrets, I can tell you, for not rethinking that whole thing before this. But I got a job at a hairdresser's in town and Daddy bought me the trailer free and clear and me and Eddie moved in and I just kept all those old ideas.

So I met Desi in the parking lot. I called him that because he talked with a funny accent but I liked him. I had my insomnia and it was about three in the morning and I went to the twenty-four-hour Wal-Mart and I was glad it was open—I'd tell that right to the face of anybody in this town—I was glad for a place to go when I couldn't sleep. So I was coming out of the store with a bag that had a little fuzzy mouse toy for Eddie, made of rabbit fur, I'm afraid, and that strikes me as pretty odd to kill all those cute little rabbits, which some people have as pets and love a lot, so that somebody else's pet of a different type can have something to play with, and it's that kind of odd thing that makes you shake your head about the way life is lived on planet Earth—Desi has helped me see things in the larger perspective—though, to be honest, it didn't stop me from buying the furry cat toy, because Eddie does love those things. Maybe today I wouldn't do the same, but I wasn't so enlightened that night when I came out of the Wal-Mart and I had that toy and some bread and baloney and a refrigerator magnet, which I collect, of a zebra head.

He was standing out in the middle of the parking lot and he wasn't moving. He was just standing still as a cow and there wasn't any car within a hundred feet of him, and, of course, his spaceship wasn't anywhere in sight, though I wasn't looking for that right away because at first glance I didn't know he was a spaceman. He was wearing a long black trench coat with the belt cinched tight and he had a black felt hat with a wide brim. Those were the things I saw first and he seemed odd, certainly, dressed like that in Bovary, but I took him for a human being, at least.

I was opening my car door and he was still standing out there and I called out to him, "Are you lost?"

His head turns my way and I still can't see him much at all except as a hat and a coat.

"Did you forget where you parked your car?" I say, and then right away I realize there isn't but about four cars total in the parking lot at that hour. So I put the bag with my things on the seat and I come around the back of the car and go a few steps toward him. I feel bad. So I call to him, kind of loud because I'm still pretty far away from him and also because I already have a feeling he might be a foreigner. I say, "I wasn't meaning to be snippy, because that's something that happens to me a lot and I can look just like you look sometimes, I'm sure, standing in the lot wondering where I am, exactly."

While I'm saying all this I'm moving kind of slow in his direction. He isn't saying anything back and he isn't moving. But already I'm noticing that his belt is cinched *very* tight, like he's got maybe an eighteen-inch waist. And as I get near, he sort of pulls his hat down to hide his face, but already I'm starting to think he's a spaceman.

I stop. I haven't seen a spaceman before except in the newspaper and I take another quick look around, just in case I missed something, like there might be four cars *and* a flying saucer. But there's nothing unusual. Then I think, Oh my, there's one place I haven't looked, and so I lift my eyes, very slow because this is something I don't want to see all the sudden, and finally I'm staring into the sky. It's a dark night and there are a bunch of stars up there and I get goose bumps because I'm pretty sure that this man standing just a few feet away is from somewhere out there. But at least there's no spaceship as big as the Wal-Mart hanging over my head with lights blinking and transporter beams ready to shine down on me. It's only stars.

So I bring my eyes down—just about as slow—to look at this man. He's still there. And in the shadow of his hat brim, with the orangey light of the parking lot all around, I can see these eyes looking at me now and they are each of them about as big as Eddie's whole head and shaped kind of like Eddie's eyes.

"Are you a spaceman?" I just say this right out.

"Yes, m'am," he says and his courtesy puts me at ease right away. Americans are courteous, my daddy says, not like your Eastern liberal New York taxi drivers.

"They haven't gone and abandoned you, have they, your friends or whoever?" I say.

"No, m'am," he says and his voice is kind of high-pitched and he has this accent, but it's more in the tone of the voice than how he says his words, like he's talking with a mouth full of grits or something.

"You looked kind of lost, is all."

"I am waiting," he says.

"That's nice. They'll be along soon, probably," I say, and I feel my feet starting to slide back in the direction of the car. There's only so far that courtesy can go in calming you down. The return of the spaceship is something I figure I can do without.

Then he says, "I am waiting for you, Edna Bradshaw."

"Oh. Good. Sure, honey. That's me. I'm Edna. Yes. Waiting for me." I'm starting to babble and I'm hearing myself like I was hovering in the air over me and I'm wanting my feet to go even faster but they seem to have stopped altogether. I wonder if it's because of some tractor beam or something. Then I wonder if they have tractor-beam pulling contests in outer space that they show on TV back in these other solar systems. I figure I'm starting to get hysterical, thinking things like that in a situation like this, but there's not much I can do about it.

He seems to know I'm struggling. He takes a tiny little step forward and his hand goes up to his hat, like he's going to take it off and hold it in front of him as he talks to me, another courtesy that even my daddy would appreciate. But his hand stops. I think he's not ready to show me his whole spaceman head. He knows it would just make things worse. His hand is bad enough, hanging there over his hat. It's got little round pads at the end of the fingers, like a gecko, and I don't stop to count them, but at first glance there just seems to be too many of them.

His hand comes back down. "I do not hurt you, Edna Bradshaw. I am a friendly guy."

"Good," I say. "Good. I figured that was so when I first saw you. Of course, you can just figure somebody around here is going to be friendly. That's a good thing about Bovary, Alabama—that's where you are, you know, though you probably do know that, though maybe not. Do you know that?"

He doesn't say anything for a moment. I'm rattling on again, and it's true I'm a little bit scared and that's why, but it's also true that I'm suddenly very sad about sounding like this to him, I'm getting some perspective on myself through his big old eyes, and I'm sad I'm making a bad impression because I want him to like me. He's sweet, really. Very courteous. Kind of boyish. And he's been waiting for me.

"Excuse me," he says. "I have been translating. You speak many words, Edna Bradshaw. Yes, I know the name of this place."

"I'm sorry. I just do that sometimes, talk a lot. Like when I get scared, which I am a little bit right now. And call me Edna."

"Please," he says, "I am calling you Edna already. And in conclusion, you have no reason to be afraid."

"I mean call me *just* Edna. You don't have to say Bradshaw every time, though my granddaddy would do that with people. He was a fountain pen salesman and he would say to people, I'm William D. Bradshaw. Call me William D. Bradshaw. And he meant it. He wanted you to say the whole name every time. But you can just call me Edna."

So the spaceman takes a step forward and my heart starts to pound something fierce, and it's not from fright, I realize, though it's some of that. "Edna," he says. "You are still afraid."

"Telling you about my granddaddy, you mean? How that's not really the point here? Well, yes, I guess so. Sometimes, if he knew you for awhile, he'd let you call him W. D. Bradshaw."

Now his hand comes up and it clutches the hat and the hat comes off and there he stands in the orange lights of the parking lot at three in the morning in my little old hometown and he doesn't have a hair on his head, though I've always liked bald men and I've read they're bald because they have so much male hormone in them, which makes them the best lovers, which would make this spaceman quite a guy, I think, and his head is pointy, kind of, and his cheeks are sunken and his cheekbones are real clear and I'm thinking already I'd like to bake some cookies for him or something, just last week I got a prize-winning recipe, off a can of cooking spray, that looks like it'd put flesh on a fencepost. And, of course, there are these big eyes of his and he blinks once, real slow, and I think it's because he's got a strong feeling in him, and he says, "Edna, my name is hard for you to say."

And I think of Desi right away, and I try it on him, and his mouth, which hasn't got anything that look like lips exactly, moves up at the edges and he makes this pretty smile.

"I have heard that name," he says. "Call me Desi. And I am waiting for you, Edna, because I study this planet and I hear you speak many words to your friends and to your subspecies companion and I detect some bright-colored aura around you and I want to meet you."

"That's good," I say, and I can feel a blush starting in my chest, where it always starts, and it's spreading up my throat and into my cheeks.

"I would like to call on you tomorrow evening, if I have your permission," he says.

"Boy," I say. "Do a lot of people have the wrong idea about spacemen. I thought you just grabbed somebody and beamed them up and that was it." It was a stupid thing to say, I realize right away. I think Desi looks a little sad to hear this. The corners of his mouth sink. "I'm sorry," I say.

"No," he says. "This is how we are perceived, it is true. You speak only the truth. This is one reason I want to meet you, Edna. You seem always to say what is inside your head without any attempt to alter it."

Now it's my turn to look a little sad, I think. But that's okay, because it gives me a chance to find out that Desi is more than courteous. His hands come out toward me at once, the little suckers on them primed to latch on to me, and I'm not even scared because I know it means he cares about me. And he's too refined to touch me this quick. His hands just hang there between us and he says, "I speak this not as a researcher but as a male creature of a parallel species."

"You mean as a man?"

His eyes blink again, real slow. "Yes. As a man. As a man I try to say that I like the way you speak."

So I give him permission to call on me and he thanks me and he turns and glides away. I know his legs are moving but he glides, real smooth, across the parking lot and I can see now that poor Desi didn't even find a pair of pants and some shoes to go with his trench coat. His legs and ankles are skinny like a frog's and his feet look a lot like his hands. But all that is unclear on the first night. He has disappeared out into the darkness and I drive on home to my subspecies companion and I tell him all about what happened while he purrs in my lap and I have two thoughts.

First, if you've never seen a cat in your entire life or anything like one and then meet a cat in a Wal-Mart parking lot in the middle of the night all covered with fur and making this rumbling noise and maybe even smelling of mouse meat, you'd have to make some serious adjustments to what you think is pretty and sweet and something you can call your own. Second—and this hits me with a little shock—Desi says he's been hearing how I talk to my friends and even to Eddie, and that sure wasn't by hanging around in his trench coat and blending in with the furniture. Of course, if you've got a spaceship that can carry you to Earth from a distant galaxy, it's not so surprising you've got some kind of radio or something that lets you listen to what everybody's saying without being there.

And when I think of this, I start to sing for Desi. I just sit for a long while where I am, with Eddie in my lap, this odd little creature that doesn't look like me at all but who I find cute as can be and who I love a lot, and I sing, because when I was a teenager I had a pretty good voice and I even thought I might be a singer of some kind, though there wasn't much call for that in Bovary except in the church choir, which is where I sang mostly, but I loved to sing other kinds of songs too. And so I say real loud, "This is for you, Desi." And then I sing every song I can think of. I sing "The Long and Winding Road" and "Lucy in the Sky with Diamonds" and "Everything Is Beautiful in Its Own Way" and a bunch of others, some twice, like "The First Time Ever I Saw Your Face." Then I do a Reba McIntire medley and I start with "Is There Life Out There" and then I do "Love Will Find Its Way to You" and "Up to Heaven" and "Long Distance Lover." I sing my heart out to Desi and I have to say this surprises me a little but maybe it shouldn't because already I'm hearing myself through his ears—though at that moment I can't even say for sure if he has ears—and I realize that a lot of what I say, I say because it keeps me from feeling so lonely.

The next night there's a knock on my door and I'm wearing my best dress, with a scoop neck, and it shows my cleavage pretty good and on the way to the door I suddenly doubt myself. I don't know if spacemen are like Earth men in that way or not. Maybe they don't appreciate a good set of knockers, especially if their women are as skinny as Desi. But I am who I am. So I put all that out of my mind and I open the door and there he is. He's got his black felt hat on, pulled down low in case any of my neighbors are watching, I figure, and he's wearing a gray pinstripe suit that's way too big for him and a white shirt and a tie with a design that's dozens of little Tabasco bottles floating around.

"Oh," I say. "You like hot food?"

This makes him stop and try to translate.

"Your tie," I say. "Don't you know about your tie?"

He looks down and lifts the end of the tie and looks at it for a little while and he is so cute doing that and so innocent-like that my heart is doing flips and I kind of wiggle in my dress a bit to make him look at who it is he's going out with. If the women on his planet are skinny, then he could be real real ready for a woman like me. That's how I figure it as I'm waiting there for him to check out his tie and be done with it, though I know it's my own fault for getting him off on that track, and me doing that is just another example of something or other.

Then Desi looks up at me, and he takes off his hat with one hand and I see that he doesn't have anything that looks like ears, really, just sort of a little dip on each side where ears might be. But that doesn't make him so odd. What's an ear mean, really? Having an ear or not having an ear won't get you to heaven, it seems to me. I look into Desi's big dark eyes and he blinks slow and then his other hand comes out from behind his back and he's got a flower for me that's got a bloom on it the color of I don't know what, a blue kind of, a red kind of, and I know this is a spaceflower of some sort and I take it from him and it weighs about as much as my Sunbeam steam iron, just this one flower.

He says, "I heard you sing for me," and he holds out his hand. If you want to know an exact count, there's eight fingers on each hand. I will end up counting them carefully later on our date, but for now there's still just a lot of fingers and I realize I'm not afraid of them anymore and I reach out to him and the little suckers latch on all over my hand, top and bottom, and it's like he's kissing me in eight different places there, over and over, they hold on to me and they pulse in each spot they touch, maybe with the beat of his heart. It's like that. And my eyes fill up with tears because this man's very fingertips are in love with me, I know.

And then he leads me to his flying saucer, which is pretty big but not as big as I imagined, not as big as all of Wal-Mart, certainly, maybe just the pharmacy and housewares departments put together. It's parked out in the empty field back of my trailer where they kept saying they'd put in a miniature golf course and they never did and you don't even see the saucer till you're right up against it, it blends in with the night, and you'd think if they can make this machine, they could get him a better suit. Then he says, "You are safe with me, Edna Bradshaw daughter of Joseph R. Bradshaw and granddaughter of William D. Bradshaw."

It later turns out these family things are important where he's from but I say to him, "William D. is dead, I only have his favorite fountain pen in a drawer somewhere, it's very beautiful, it's gold and it looks like that Chrysler Building in New York, and you should forget about Joseph R. for the time being because I'm afraid you and my daddy aren't going to hit it off real well and I just as soon not think about that till I have to."

Then Desi smiles at me and it's because of all those words, and especially me talking so blunt about my daddy, and I guess also about my taking time to tell him about the beautiful fountain pen my granddaddy left for me, but there's reasons I talk like this, I guess, and Desi says he came to like me from hearing me talk.

Listen to me even now. I'm trying to tell this story of Desi and me and I can't help myself going on about every little thing. But the reasons are always the same, and it's true I'm lonely again. And it's true I'm scared again because I've been a fool.

Desi took me off in his spaceship and we went out past the moon and I barely had time to turn around and look back and I wanted to try to figure out where Bovary was but I hadn't even found the U.S.A. when everything got blurry and before you know it we were way out in the middle of nowhere, out in space, and I couldn't see the sun or the moon or anything close up, except all the stars were very bright, and I'm not sure whether we were moving or not because there was nothing close enough by to tell, but I think we were parked, like this was the spaceman's version of the dead-end road to the rock quarry, where I kissed my first boy. I turned to Desi and he turned to me and I should've been scared but I wasn't. Desi's little suckers were kissing away at my hand and then we were kissing on the lips except he didn't have any but it didn't make any difference because his mouth was soft and warm and smelled sweet, like Binaca breath spray, and I wondered if he got that on Earth or if it was something just like Binaca that they have on his planet as well.

Then he took me back to his little room on the spaceship and we sat on things like beanbag chairs and we talked a long time about what life in Bovary is like and what life on his planet is like. Desi is a research scientist, you see. He thinks that the only way for our two peoples to learn about each other is to meet and to talk and so forth. There are others where he lives that think it's best just to use their machines to listen in and do their research like that, on the sly. There are even a bunch of guys back there who say forget the whole thing, leave them to hell alone. Let everybody stick to their own place. And I told Desi that my daddy would certainly agree with the leave-them-the-hell-alone guys from his planet, but I agreed with him.

It was all very interesting and very nice, but I was starting to get a little sad. Finally I said to Desi, "So is this thing we're doing here like research? You asked me out as part of a scientific study? I was called by the Gallup Poll people once and I don't remember what it was about but I answered 'none of the above' and 'other' to every question."

For all the honesty Desi said he admired in me, I sure know it wasn't anything to do with my answers to a Gallup

Poll that was bothering me, but there I was, bogged down talking about all of that, and that's a land of dishonesty, it seems to me now.

But he knew what I was worried about. "No, Edna," he says. "There are many on my planet who would be critical of me. They would say this is why we should have no contact at all with your world. Things like this might happen."

He pauses right there and as far as I know he doesn't have anything to translate and I swallow hard at the knot in my throat and I say, "Things like what?"

Then both his hands take both my hands and when you've got sixteen cute little suckers going at you, it's hard to make any real tough self-denying kind of decisions and that's when I end up with a bona fide spaceman lover. And enough said, as we like to end touchy conversations around the hair-dressing parlor, except I will tell you that he was bald all over and it's true what they say about bald men.

Then he takes me to the place where he picked the flower. A moon of some planet or other and there's only these flowers growing as far as the eye can see in all directions and there are clouds in the sky and they are the color of Eddie's turds after a can of Nine Lives Crab and Tuna, which just goes to show that even in some far place in another solar system you can't have everything. But maybe Desi likes those clouds and maybe I'd see it that way too sometime, except I may not have that chance now, though I could've, it's my own damn fault, and if I've been sounding a little bit hit-and-miss and here-and-there in the way I've been telling all this, it's now you find out why.

Desi and I stand in that field of flowers for a long while, his little suckers going up and down my arm and all over my throat and chest, too, because I can tell you that a space-man does too appreciate a woman who has some flesh on her, especially in the right places, but he also appreciates a woman who will speak her mind. And I was standing there wondering if I should tell him about those clouds or if I should just keep my eyes on the flowers and my mouth shut. Then he says, "Edna, it is time to go."

So he takes my hand and we go back into his spaceship and he's real quiet all the sudden and so am I because I know the night is coming to an end. Then before you know it, there's Earth right in front of me and it's looking, even out there, pretty good, pretty much like where I should be, like my own flower box and my own propane tank and my own front Dutch door look when I drive home at night from work.

Then we are in the field behind the house and it seems awful early in the evening for as much as we've done, and later on I discover it's like two weeks later and Desi had some other spaceman come and feed Eddie while we were gone, though he should have told me because I might've been in trouble at the hairdressing salon, except they be-lieved me pretty quick when I said a spaceman had taken me off, because that's what they'd sort of come around to thinking themselves after my being gone without a trace for two weeks and they wanted me to tell the newspaper about it because I might get some money for it, though I'm not into anything for the money, though my daddy says it's only

American to make money any way you can, but I'm not *that* American, it seems to me, especially if my daddy is right about what American is, which I suspect he's not.

What I'm trying to say is that Desi stopped in this other field with me, this planet-Earth field with plowed-up ground and witchgrass all around and the smell of early summer in Alabama, which is pretty nice, and the sound of cicadas sawing away in the trees and something like a kind of hum out on the horizon, a nighttime sound I listen to once in a while and it makes me feel like a train whistle in the distance makes me feel, which I also listen for, especially when I'm lying awake with my insomnia and Eddie is sleeping near me, and that hum out there in the distance is all the wide world going about its business and that's good but it makes me glad I'm in my little trailer in Bovary, Alabama, and I'll know every face I see on the street the next morning.

And in the middle of a field full of all that, what was I to say when Desi took my hand and asked me to go away with him? He said, "I have to return to my home planet now and after that go off to other worlds. I am being transferred and I will not be back here. But Edna, we feel love on my planet just like you do here. That is why I know it is right that we learn to speak to each other, your people and mine. And in conclusion, I love you, Edna Bradshaw. I want you to come away with me and be with me forever."

How many chances do you have to be happy? I didn't even want to go to Mobile, though I wasn't asked, that's true enough, and I wouldn't have been happy there anyway. So that doesn't count as a blown chance. But this one was

different. How could I love a spaceman? How could I be
happy in a distant galaxy? These were questions that I
had to answer right away, out in the smell of an Alabama
summer with my cat waiting for me, though I'm sure he
could've gone with us, that wasn't the issue, and with my
daddy living just on the other side of town, though, to tell
the truth, I wouldn't miss him much, the good Lord forgive
me for that sentiment, and I did love my spaceman, I knew
that, and I still do, I love his wiggly hairless shy courteous
smart-as-a-whip self. But there's only so many new things a
person can take in at once and I'd about reached my limit
on that night.

So I heard myself say, "I love you too, Desi. But I can't
leave the planet Earth. I can't even leave Bovary."

That's about all I could say. And Desi didn't put up a fuss
about it, didn't try to talk me out of it, though now I wish to
God he'd tried, at least tried, and maybe he could've done
it, cause I could hear myself saying these words like it wasn't
me speaking, like I was standing off a ways just listening in.
But my spaceman was shy from the first time I saw him. And
I guess he just didn't have it in him to argue with me, once
he felt I'd rejected him.

That's the way the girls at the hairdressing salon see it.

I guess they're right. I guess they're right, too, about telling the newspaper my story. Maybe some other spaceman
would read it, somebody from Desi's planet, and maybe
Desi's been talking about me and maybe he'll hear about
how miserable I am now and maybe I can find him or he
can find me.

Because I am miserable. I haven't even gone near my daddy for a few months now. I look around at the people in the streets of Bovary and I get real angry at them, for some reason. Still, I stay right where I am. I guess now it's because it's the only place he could ever find me, if he wanted to. I go out into the field back of my trailer at night and I walk all around it, over and over, each night, I walk around and around under the stars because a spaceship only comes in the night and you can't even see it until you get right up next to it.

"JFK Secretly Attends Jackie Auction"

When we turned onto Seventy-second Street and saw what awaited us, my handler flinched, and he tightened his grip on the wheel. I suspect he wanted to accelerate on by and abort the whole plan. But he knew the Director had okayed it and he looked at me.

"Are you sure, Mr. President?" he said.

The only thing you could see of Sotheby's was a white awning. The front of the building had completely disappeared behind television trucks and satellite dishes. It was a risk, of course. But things that Jackie and I had lived with were disappearing into the hands of strangers, and it made me feel as if I were dead. The CIA could get me in only on this third day, and I knew well enough already that the four thousand dollars I'd been able to scrape together from my ration of pocket money probably wouldn't allow me to buy back even a tie clip. But there were other things working on me. I had to go.

We passed an NHK satellite truck beaming to Tokyo and then a BBC truck, and I said to my handler, "Let every nation know, whether it wishes us well or ill, that we shall pay any price."

"Mr. President?" he said, pressing me to prove I wasn't rambling. He was a very young man.

"You probably never even read my inaugural address," I said.

He was reaching for his cellular phone.

"Dave, you don't have to call. I'm just having a little joke. It's all right. The Director and I talked it over. There's no better place to hide than the glare."

Dave pulled his hand back to the steering wheel. "I'm sorry, Mr. President."

"That's okay, Dave. In case of domestic insurrection, the president has contingency plans to go to a safe house in Arlington, Virginia."

His hand went for the phone again.

"Chill out, Dave. That was President Johnson's plan. Old news. I said that on purpose as a joke."

"I respectfully request that you don't joke like that, Mr. President."

My handler is right to be nervous. After all, loose talk is why I'm in the position of having to sneak into the public auction of the effects of my late wife. It's why my long-suffering

Jackie was led to live, unaware, as a bigamist, the wife of a Greek who had a face that could stop a thousand ships.

The bullets fired on that fateful afternoon in Dallas killed only the editor in my brain. After that moment, I could not hold my tongue about anything. I woke up on the gurney rolling into the hospital and began at once to disclose all the state secrets of that very secretive time. Of no use now. But it's far too late to explain any of this to a world that the Agency determined quite quickly must never have even momentary access to me.

I completely agreed with the decision. It's only the editor that's gone. My powers to reason are still completely intact, and this was the only reasonable course. Anyone who came near me would become a security risk. And of no import to the CIA but critical to me, I would have talked endlessly to Jackie about the things that we agreed would never be spoken. Along with the secret details of our foreign policy, the smells and sights and tastes of all the women I'd ever known would come tumbling out. There was no choice but to bury the wax dummy in my place. Not only is my faculty of reason untouched, so are my powers to remember. Sweet memory. It's been the great comfort of my confinement.

Still, I'm very glad now to be sliding to a stop in front of this white awning. I know I can meet my commitment to silence. I realize that it's still important. I say that what I know is of no use. But I suspect that if I were to speak now of the doomsday rocket silo twenty miles north by northeast of Burgdorf, Idaho, in the Gospel Hump Wilderness, I would be speaking of something still in place, though perhaps the target agenda of Moscow, Peking, Pyongyang, and Hanoi would have changed slightly. But I am determined to withhold even the faintest allusion to these things.

As I pointed out to the Director, I never asked to go to the funerals or the weddings. I didn't ask to go to Teddy when he left that girl in the dark water at Chappaquiddick or to my nephew, who never even had a chance to know me, when it was clear to me that he needed to speak honestly of what he'd done to that girl in Florida. I didn't even ask to go to John-John to warn him about the magazine business. But this auction was a different thing.

I step out of the car. I suspect the Director has watchers in the crowd. I am never out of sight. But for a moment I feel alive again. I feel that I am living in my body, in the present moment. How sweet that is, I've come to realize in these thirty-two years of exile. How often in the life I used to lead was I in a place that could have filled me with memories, but my mind carried me elsewhere. I missed the moment. Now, on the sidewalk in front of Sotheby's, I head to the end of a long line of people whose faces once would have turned to me, whose hands would have come out to touch me. It took me a long time to get used to that touching. I never quite did. But I crave it now. They touch me now in my dreams. Hands trembling faintly from excitement, warm with the flush of desire. I touch them back, each one.

But here, the TV lights glare and the crowds line up and they yearn to touch only the things I touched. I think this is similar to what Abraham Lincoln dreamed the week before he was killed. He dreamed that he awoke from a deep sleep and he heard distant sobbing. He arose and made his way through the empty hallways of the White House to the East Room, where he found a great catafalque draped in black. A military guard stood there and Lincoln asked, "Who is dead?" The man replied, "It is the President." I could ask anyone now in this line, "Whose French silver-plated toothbrush box with cover is this, being auctioned off to strangers?" And the reply would be, "It is the President's."

I pass all these hands stuffed in pockets or clutching purses or fluttering in conversation. I pass all these faces turned away from this bearded man with close-cropped hair and the faint line of a scar on the side of his skull and the hobble of a very bad back. And I know I should be glad that there is not the tiniest flicker of recognition. The Director and I are in complete agreement. He's stuck his neck out for me. Pity for an old man and his past. Trust that old age has slowed my tongue, which it has, somewhat. But part of me is ready to tell, at the slightest glance from a stranger, how Mayor Richard Daley found fourteen thousand votes in the cemeteries of Chicago to swing a state and elect a president. And I would point out the debt of gratitude the whole planet owes those dead voters. None of us knew at the time of the missile crisis of 1962 that the Soviet general in charge of troops in Cuba was authorized to use tactical nuclear weapons. After the Soviet Union broke up, the general appeared on TV—I get all the cable channels—and he said if the American President had chosen to send troops to the island, they would have been nuked. If Richard Nixon had been the President, he certainly would have sent those

troops. What does this mean? It means those dead Chicago-
ans prevented a nuclear holocaust. My impulse to talk about
these things aside, credit should be given to this necropolis
of American heroes.

But no stranger gives me a glance. I go to the end of the
line and my back is hurting, but out here in public, the pain
reassures me somehow. A woman up ahead in the line turns
her face idly toward me. She has hair the color of the old Red
Grange model football we used in Hyannis the same autumn
I made love on the overstuffed chair in my Senate office,
to a woman who was all bones and freckles and teeth and
her thick hair was the same color, a roan color, and she sat
on my lap and thrashed her hair around me. She has spent
time with me often these past years, in my memory. And
this woman in line turns her eyes briefly to me and then her
attention passes on. She is perhaps thirty-five. In my memory
I am thirty-five, but this woman before me now sees only an
old man. But I'm still sitting on that overstuffed chair and the
leather squeaks beneath me and I'm sweating and smelling
the woman's hair and I tell her about its color, the color of
a Red Grange football, and she laughs. The woman in line
laughs now. She is with someone near her, but I don't look
to see who it is. I watch her face dilate sweetly in laughter
and if she were standing next to me, I know I would speak
to her of this other woman, whose name I can't remember
and whose eyes I can't remember, though I've often tried
in these years of exile. I would like to remember her eyes,
because remembering these other things as vividly as I do
makes me feel as if the memory of her eyes should be there

too but it got put aside and then sold off or given away and it was a big mistake. I want it back.

I want my Harvard-crest cufflinks back, too. I'm thinking of them as I finally make it through the front door of Sotheby's and a young Negro woman in a uniform holds out her hand to help me through the metal detector. I would not call her a Negro to her face—I know the language has changed—but I am still a creature of my time and Martin called himself that. I will always remember where I was on the day Martin was shot. I was in the little stone-walled garden in the cottage in the compound in Virginia. I was about to launch a putt across the fifteen-foot green whose one hole has pulled me to it ten thousand times a year for all these years. I was just aligning the head of my putter—I want my old putter back, too, by the way, though it's sure to draw a small fortune—I was just squaring up the head of my putter when whatever aide it was assigned to me at that time—I don't remember him except that he was young—stepped out of the back door and he said "Mr. President" with a rasp in his throat and I knew that it was something terrible. Poor Martin. How nice it would have been if only his editor had been shot away and they thought to bring him to me. We could have told each other so many things we never had sense enough to talk about when we were living our public lives. And Bobby too. We three could live together and I'd talk with Martin and I'd wrestle my little brother to the ground—even with my back—and with his editor shot off Bobby could tell me what he really thinks of me, and that would do him good.

So this young Negro woman reaches out to the old man she sees in front of her, an old man having trouble straightening up, having just gone up some steps with a very bad back, and her hand clutches me beneath my forearm. And though there are two sleeves between me and her flesh, I thrill at her touch. I straighten up, not wanting her to be touching the arm of a stooping old man, and there must be pain but I don't feel it. She looks me in the eyes, just before I step through, and I think there is some flicker of recognition there.

"Do you know me?" I ask.

"No sir," she says.

I realize I'm on the verge of telling her about the perfect hit man we'd hired to kill Fidel Castro in 1963. Pedro Antonelli. I don't know why I think she'd be interested in this. But I know I'm not supposed to say anything. So I step through the arch of the metal detector, and the machine cries out as if it had seen a ghost. The woman who touched my arm is beside me and I'm ready to confess.

But before I can speak, she says, "Do you have anything metal, sir?" and I understand.

I tap the side of my head, on the tight ridge of scar tissue, and I say, "Metal plate. From service for my country." I think she can hear the ring of it beneath my knuckle.

"I'm sorry, sir," she says, and I'm hoping she will reach up to touch the place herself. But her hand goes to my arm again and urges me toward a desk. "Thank you," she says. "Show your registration slip over there."

I move away from her and there is still a ringing in my head and at the desk they give me my bidding card, and from the push of people behind me I'm going up more steps, made of stone, and my back is hurting again and I'm growing older by the moment, though I can still feel her touch on my arm.

The Director has not been very good in recognizing my desires as a man. I've always understood the risks. There weren't very many women with the highest Agency clearances who were prepared to open themselves to me. One or two over the years. And there was always a drug to slow my tongue, because even the highest clearance is still bound tight by the need-to-know test. I presume the rest of me was slowed as well by the drug, certainly my awareness was, for I remember these women only very faintly. I wish there had been another way, a safer way, a fully conscious way, for me to feel the touch of a woman. But I did not ask what more they could do for me. I only asked what I could do for my country.

The room is very large and I struggle toward the front, but the rows of padded beige chairs are filled more than halfway back already. I look around and I straighten again, this time with clear pain, but a pain put aside. I see Jackie down the row. She has not yet sat down. She has a pillbox hat and that stiff bouffant hairdo. But I remind myself that she couldn't be that young. And she's dead. I look again. Her eyes—she is smoothing her hot-pink dress and looking around the room—her eyes are Asian. Her gaze fixes and hardens and I follow it and coming down the aisle is another Jackie, a Caucasian one, dressed in mint blue, unaware still of her rival.

I sit. I am on the aisle and breathing heavily. I suspect there are several of me in the room as well, though I hope not to catch even a brief sight of them. I can't help but look up, and the second Jackie, with a slightly longer hairdo, twirled up at the bottom, brushes past me. Her face turns and her eyes fall and she looks straight at me. She doesn't show any sign at all of sensing who I am. As false as she is—her eyes are much too close together and her mouth is too thin—I'm briefly disappointed that she doesn't recognize me. I look away and I close my eyes. Jackie has been with me, as well, all these years.

When John and Caroline were sleeping in the afternoons, I'd clear half an hour in the affairs of state and tell my staff to leave us alone, and Jackie and I would make love in the room where they all made love, the presidents of the United States. And I'd ask her to talk to me about art while we touched. I wanted her mind in this act, and her voice, breathy as a starlet. I've been slandered over and over in the books. Smathers was way out of line telling those things about our Senate bachelor days. I might've talked like that about women with him—men have always talked stupidly about women with each other. And it's true that my mind was often elsewhere when I touched the women who always seemed to be there, open to me. But not because I didn't value them. Not because they were objects to me, taken up and cast off even more coldly than the objects for sale in this crowded room. There are suddenly too many things in my head at once. This happens sometimes. The voice of a woman now. "New bidder on my right at sixty thousand." I don't know what it is that's for sale but I have only four thousand and I clench inside, a little desperate for a reason I can't quite identify. Jackie would rise naked above me as I lay delicately still, trying not to let my back distract me. She would rise into a column of sunlight from the window and her skin was dusky and her voice was soft and she would be wearing a single strand of pearls, the only thing left on her body, and she would speak of the geometry of Attic pottery in the tenth century B.C., and the bands of decoration were drawn in black on cream-colored clay and there would be meanders and chevrons and swastikas and then, gradually, as the ninth century B.C. passed and the eighth began, there was an advent of animal forms. She spoke of all these wonderful vessels: the amphora with its two great handles and the krater with its fat belly and wide mouth and the skinny lekythos, for pouring. Jackie would throw her head back and her mind would make my breath catch and now the eighth century B.C. was in full flower with horsemen and chariots and battle scenes crowding these clay pots, and scenes of men and women lamenting the dead, and her eyes would tear up, even as we touched and she fell forward and I put my hands on her back and felt her bones.

"No, m'am, it's not your bid." A long, sweetly handsome face, a Boston sort of face, to my eye, is floating over the lectern at the front of the room, rolling out numbers. "It's at a hundred and ten on the phone. Now a hundred and twenty in the front. Yes, m'am, now it's yours, at a hundred and thirty. A hundred and thirty thousand dollars. A hundred and forty at the back of the room." I look away from her and I think for a moment that it must be a Grecian krater for sale, something

I'd always hoped Onassis would buy for her but that she would never speak of with him. Then on a TV monitor to the side of the room I see a triple strand of pearls. A hundred and forty and now fifty and now sixty and I squeeze my eyes shut. Jackie crosses the White House bedroom to me, her clothes strewn behind her and the pearls tight at her throat, and they make her nakedness astonishing to me, as if no woman has ever been this naked before, and it takes the contrast, the failed covering of the thin string of pearls, to show me this.

The room has burst into applause. I look up. And the second Jackie, her eyes too close together but rather large, very dark, is looking at me. She is in the aisle seat directly across from me and she is looking at me intently.

"Now lot number 454A," the woman at the front says.

This Jackie in blue won't look away. She knows me. She knows.

"A single-strand, simulated-pearl necklace and ear clips."

I drag my attention away from the simulated Jackie's gaze and on the TV screen is the necklace my wife wears in my memories of our lovemaking. Perhaps not that very one. Perhaps some other necklace. She wore a single strand of pearls at our wedding, too. When Jackie wore pearls, I felt her nakedness always, even beneath her clothes. I stare at this necklace on the television screen and it could well be the pearls of any of a hundred memories I've taken out and handled on countless nights of what has been my life. I feel myself rise up slightly, briefly, from my chair. I hold back my hands which want to lift to the screen, to this image of her pearls. I want these pearls very badly.

"The opening bid is ten thousand dollars," the woman with the long face says.

I cry out. My cry is in anguish, but there are twenty cries at the same moment and they are all saying "Ten thousand." So no one hears. Except perhaps the Jackie across the aisle. This necklace is beyond my reach already. All the fragments of my life in this place are beyond my reach. I look to the right and she is fixed on me, this thin-lipped faux first lady. Her mouth moves.

I stand up, I turn, I drop my bidding card and push my heavy legs forward, the pain in my back flaring at each step. Twenty thousand. Thirty. The bidders' hands fly up, flashing their cards, the dollars pursue me up the aisle. Forty thousand from the phones. Fifty from the front row. I touch her there, at the hollow of her throat just below the pearls. Jackie rises up straight, nestled naked on the center of me, and I lift my hand and put my fingertips on the hollow of her throat. And I am out the main door of the auction room, breaking through a hedge of reporters who pay no attention to me. I stop, my chest heaving and the pain spreading all through me, and I look over my shoulder and just before the reporters close back up, I see her. She's coming toward me. The Jackie in blue has risen and is following.

The bodies of newsmen intervene but I know she will soon be here. Now I wish for the Director's men. I want their hands to take my elbows and I want them to whisper, This way, Mr. President, and I want them to carry me away, back to the empty garden and a patch of sunlight where I can just sit and sort out the strange things going on inside me. But I am on my own, it seems. The main staircase is before me, but there are more reporters that way and the faux Jackie will catch me just in time for them.

I turn blindly to the right, I go along a corridor, my face lowered, trying to disappear, and another staircase is before me, a modest one, linoleum, a metal handrail. My hand goes out to it, I take one step down and her voice is in my ear.

"Please," she says.

I stop.

"I recognized you," she says.

I turn to her.

"But I didn't mean to drive you away."

Her eyes are very beautiful. The brown of them, like the earth in the deepest hole you could dig for yourself, like a place to bury yourself and sleep forever, is like the brown of Jackie's eyes. I want to tell her secrets. About myself. About missile silos. About anything. All the secrets I know.

"I thought I read somewhere you were dead," she says.

She sounds charmingly ironic to me. But there is something about her eyes now, a little unfocused. And she is dressed as my wife, who is dead.

"I didn't believe it," she says.

"Good," I say, struggling with my voice which wants to speak much more.

Then she says, "I've seen all your movies."

There is a stopping in me.

"*The Grapes of Wrath* is my favorite."

"Thank you," I say. "Hurry back to the auction now. You must buy some of Jackie's pearls."

She tilts her head at the intensity of my advice.

I turn away from her, move myself down the steps.

"Yes," she calls after me. "I will."

I am out the side entrance now, on York Avenue. It is quieter here. No one looks at me. I am a ghost again. I turn and walk away, I don't know in what direction.

But this I do know: I love Jackie. I know because inside me I have her hands and her hair and her nipples and her toes and her bony elbows and knees and her shoes and belts and scarves and her shadow and her laugh and her moans and her simulated-pearl necklaces and her yellow gypsy bangle bracelets and her Gorham silver heart-shaped candy dish and her silver-plated salt and pepper shakers. And somebody has my golf clubs. And somebody has my cigar humidor. And somebody has my Harvard crest cuff links. And somebody has a single strand of Jackie's pearls, a strand that I also have. And what is it about all these things of a person that won't fade away? The things you seek out over and over and you look at intently and you touch. You touch with your own hands. Or you touch with the silent movement of your mind in the long and solitary night. Surely these things are signs of love. In a world where we don't know how to stay close to each other, we try to stay close to these things. In a world where death comes unexpectedly and terrifies us as the ultimate act of forgetting, we try to remember so that we can overcome death. And so we go forth together in love and in peace and in deep fear, my fellow Americans, Jackie and I and all of you. And you have my undying thanks.

"*Titanic* Survivors Found in Bermuda Triangle"

The cold air hanging in this room, it feels like the North Atlantic. Not nearly so cold as that, really, but so surprisingly cold on this hot summer day that it has the same shock to it as the air on that night where the greater part of me continues to dwell, and I move to this place on the wall and the air is rushing in and I pull back away from it, it feels like a gash there, a place ripped open by ice and letting all this cold air rush in. Cold. I was so cold in the boat, and before me was this vast interruption of the sea, of the night, ablaze at a thousand places on it with spots of light and the smoke still slithered up from its stacks and for a moment the lights struck me as the lives still there on the boat and then the smoke struck me as the souls of those lives departing already, climbing to heaven from this death that was falling even at that moment upon the bodies, though in fact there was no one dead yet, probably, unless it were some poor engine room workers whom the vast jagged wall of ice sought out at once, in that first moment of the calamity, a moment I recognized instantly, perhaps even before the captain of the ship did, damn fool of an arrogant man he must have been, a man, of course, and me a scorned woman bullied in the streets of London only a few days before by men who would not let us speak, much less gain the vote. But this woman knew what had happened to this man's ship with the first faint shudder and the distant hard cry of the hull.

Now I am in this room in a place and time as foreign to me as the planet Mars, which has canals and civilized life, if Percival Lowell the noted astronomer of the distinguished Lowell family of Massachusetts is to be believed, and I read his book as a teenager, in 1895, a book given to me by my father, who put the story on his front page—*The New York World Ledger* declared "Life Possible on Planet Mars"—and I did believe, so if I can believe there is life on Mars, then why am I still slow in believing in the reality of this hotel room in a year decades removed from the night when I fled a ship and then fell into a deep sleep? Perhaps the problem is the fear I have of this room, for it has this gash and the cold air pours in and I worry that the room will fill and it will sink.

I am alone. From what I understand—and "understand" is a relative word now, and surely not just for me in an era like this, though more so for me, of course—I understand that I am alone in some surpassing way, plucked out of a place in the sea that apparently is notorious for mysteries, a place far from the fatal ice field, and I have outlived by many years everyone I ever knew and I am still just turned thirty. Not that I wasn't alone even on that night in April in 1912. It was a matter of pride to me, and would have been to any of my friends, all of them women who knew that we have a higher calling than the world had ever allowed for us, and who could travel alone as well as any man. I went to London to attend the convention of the National Union of Women's Suffrage Societies, the English edition of our own National American Woman Suffrage Association birthed from the loins of our great Susan B. Anthony and Elizabeth Cady Stanton and Lucy Stone, all heroines in my time, all women who'd known how to be alone.

I am afraid to bathe. The place is so bright and so hard-surfaced, but the sense of utter strangeness about the design of things is starting to wear off. It's the water. It flows so quickly, so profusely. I watch it run hard into the tub and it seems out of control and I stop the water and open the drain and I think of a man whose name I do not even know. For there was something more specific, more personal, in the scene before me as I sat in the lifeboat on that night. The lights and the smoke, I truly did feel them directly, as if they were the desperate souls on that ship, but to me they were humanity generalized, they were the masses. I have a mind. That's something else a woman has in equal measure with a man. And I was inclined, in the use of my mind, to think and speak often of the masses. I was no Marxist, though I had read his books, and though I was occasionally accused of being one

by some stupid man or other, and though my father's newspaper might well have run a headline "All of Human History
Redefined" and been close to the truth, I think. We were
moving into the century that would carry humanity to a new
millennium and everything was being made new. But I have
been sitting on this remarkable bed that can be commanded
to have a life of its own, quaking gently at the touch of a knob,
and I have become conscious of the pattern of my mind, how
it has always been easy for me to think of humanity as just
that, a monolithic thing, or at best a bipartite thing, men and
women. Yes, women too. I strove for the rights of women and
how often I thought of them—of myself, too, therefore, in a
way—as a large thing made up only incidentally of individu-
als, important only because of the concerns that were held in
common, a corporate entity.

This man seemed stupid at first, in a typical way, when
I met him on the promenade deck not long after we struck
the iceberg. He was English and he was stiff but he had very
nice eyes, which I could see only by moonlight for a long
while, but they were soft really, a woman's eyes. I sat in the
lifeboat and watched the *Titanic* and its bow was gone and
the rest was beginning to lift, though slowly, the motion not
quite visible, but inexorable, clearly so. The great propellers
at the rear were exposed, like a sexual part normally hidden
from polite view but naked now in the throes of this powerful feeling. And he was standing up there on the boat deck,
invisible to me since our boat had been lowered away, but
his eyes were searching the sea for me even then, I knew. He
was happy I was safe. Why had I let him persuade me to live?

I was reading in my cabin and I heard the sound and felt the faint hesitation in this great beast of a ship. I put my book down and I was instantly angry. They had appeared in the newspapers in London, an array of mustachioed men with derbies saying that this ship was the technological wonder of the age, a testament to man's power over the elements, a vast machine, greater than any in history, and indestructible, unsinkable. I'd known even then that it was all an age-old lie. But I booked passage. I was anxious to get back to New York. The convention had led to the streets and we had marched to Trafalgar Square and the crowds had lined up and they had mostly jeered us and the bobbies had ringed us in and prodded us gently with their sticks and isolated us in small groups and then talked to us with unctuous voices as if we were children, and we drifted away. We took it. There were some angry words and there were a few latchings on to gas lamps and iron fence posts and some arrests and a few flashed fingernails drawing a little bobby blood, though not by me.

To be honest, I grew weary of it all suddenly, and I went away. I cashed in my passage back to America and I went off to Italy for a little while, to Venice. I rented a room in a palazzo on the Rio San Luca and I found a small campo nearby with a fountain and a statue of the Virgin Mary without her child in hand, just her, and I sat in the sun, dressed from throat to ankle in a shirtwaist suit and I read and I spoke to no one. At night I would lie on the bed and the window would be open and I would read some more, by candlelight, still in my clothes, and one night there was a full moon and I went out and the tide was high and I think there had been storms at sea and I wandered the dark paths toward the Piazza San Marco and I came through the gallery and suddenly before me was the piazza and it was covered with water from the lagoon. Thinly, but there was not a single stone left uncovered. I drew back. The moon was shimmering out there in the water, and the stars, and I was afraid. And I was suddenly conscious of my solitariness there in that place, in that city, in that country, in the world. I had friends but we only had ideas between us and though the ideas were strong and righteous, I had not yet been naked in Venice except curled tight in a stone room with a tub of water and a sponge, wiping the scent of my body away, and quickly, never looking at myself, and then rushing back into my clothes. For all my ideas I was not comfortable in this woman's body.

And worse, it had its own intent: I felt a stirring in me at San Marco, a thing more like a need than a desire, a thing that I did not agree with but that would hear no arguments, no matter how clear and reasonable. Still, though I could not persuade it, I could put it aside. And I left the piazza, my mind ascendant, without so much as making my feet naked and wading out into this liquid sky. Instead I went back to my room and then back to London and I hated these men who'd made this ship but I have learned to wait for justice in this life, I have learned that there is always a long and perhaps even endless wait for justice, and so when I bought my ticket I did not expect the arrogance of these men to be so quickly punished. And then the moment came and I knew what it was and I went up onto the promenade deck and he was there looking out at the sea. He was tall and dressed in tweeds and he had a mustache, but he had no hat and he was watching the icebergs out there in the calm and moonlit sea and I wanted to tell him what I knew.

So I came near him and I said, "We're doomed now."

Then he turned his face to me and his eyes were soft and I would be patient with him for the sake of his woman's eyes, I thought.

He said something about the ship being all right, this unsinkable ship. I wondered if he really believed that. I said, "We've struck an iceberg. The deed is done."

Then he looked back out to the ice. I realized he was, in fact, listening to me. He was changing his opinion.

"And suppose we have," he said, a gravity in his voice now. I felt a rustle of something in me before this man who was listening, a sweet feeling, even a legitimate one, I thought. But it's then that he played the fool. He asked me if I was traveling alone and he tried to blame my fears on that.

When the sound of hammering and the thrashing of air woke me from a deep dreamless sleep, I naturally expected to find myself in the ice field on the morning of April 15, 1912. But overhead was an astonishing thing, a great dark machine, hovering. I thought of the Martians. For a long while. Even after this machine had suddenly swung away and dashed off. Then there was another sharp sound and a ship was approaching and I realized that the air was quite warm and this ship had towers and attachments that were strange to me, like no ship I had ever seen. Some of the others in the lifeboat, women, of course—we were the ones saved with only a few male crew members to row—some of the women in the boat began to weep with fear. "Quiet!" I cried out to them. "Keep your dignity." And I understood that my anger at them was like their tears. I was frightened into a feeling that I wanted to repudiate as not truly my own.

But when the ship eased up to us and we were finally on its deck and safe, the captain of the vessel, dressed in a white uniform, came to us where we were huddled. And it was a woman. "I am Captain O'Brien," she said and I knew at once that we had somehow passed far into a future time. I imagined my father's paper proclaiming "Woman Captains Ship" and soon, of course, there were more wonders. "Great Silver Airship Carries People Five Miles Above Earth," for instance, and "Horses Disappear from Roads, Replaced Universally by Racing Cars" and "Mathematical Genius Transferred to Tiny Machine" and "Window on World in Every Home." I have been in this hotel room in Washington, D.C., for less than an hour now and I am very weary. But I have looked through that window, and its view will change to a different part of the world with the merest touch on a small planchette in my hand. This brings a heady feeling of power and I found I could rest on no image for more than a few moments, there is too much to see, and as a result I have seen almost nothing, clearly. My head began to spin and I closed the window. I know I speak in something of a metaphor. It's not a window but one more machine, a thing called television. And perhaps all these machines, all this technology, mean that the men in mustaches and derby hats triumphed at last. Perhaps ships no longer sink. But through this television I've seen enough images of women intimately involved with machines to believe that we've been enfranchised in the creation of technology, as well. I am happy for that, but the feeling is not unadulterated. I have to face this selfish part of me.

I am no longer needed, for one thing. I have no proof of it, but I am certain in a world like this that women have the right to vote. And I am confident, too, that politicians have become honest and responsive, as a result. And if there is a woman ship captain and if we have been enfranchised, then I can even expect that there have been women presidents of the United States. It is selfish, but this makes me sad. It would have been better to have died in my own time.

But he saved me, this nameless man. With all the wonders I've seen and the losses I've realized since I woke from my long and mysterious sleep, it is this man who will not let go of my mind. And there are clothes laid out for me on the bed, strange clothes, a skirt and shirtwaist and undergarments that are skimpy and loose and I am not used to my body, what am I to do with my body now that the focus of my mind has been rendered obsolete? But this is not simply a problem of the new age. Indeed, if in my own time I'd been more comfortable in that fleshy self, I would perhaps have a function, or at least a prospect of pleasure, before me now.

I wish I'd stayed on the ship with him. But I didn't even know his name. Even after I saw through his foolishness. He tried to convince me that what I knew about the ship was attributable to my being a woman traveling alone, but when

I challenged him, when I told him that I knew what death was about, he listened to me again. When I was a child— dear God, more than a century ago now—and my father was editor of the *Mingo County Courier* in West Virginia and going up even then against the coal company excesses, there was a mine collapse near where we lived and I went with my father to the place, and as soon as I entered that town, I could feel the death in the air, on my skin, all over my body. When I remember it now, it feels like what a man might feel like, stealing in on you in the night and touching you against your will, only you're sleeping and he's touching you very lightly so that he doesn't wake you. And there was a smell in the air. Maybe not quite perceptible but you felt it coming in through your nose and into your lungs, filling you up.

It was that way on the *Titanic*. As soon as I stepped onto the deck, though almost no one knew what I knew and they were going about their lives, I could smell that same smell. To feel those things on my skin and in my lungs when I was a child, and to watch, as I did, the women of that mining town clutching each other, helpless: I don't think the world was the same for me after that. But I didn't speak of that to the man on the promenade deck. I just told him about the mine disaster and what I smelled and that I smelled it again. For almost any man, this would not convince him at all. He would use those very intuitions against me. But he listened, and then he said he was sorry. He actually apologized, and I knew he meant it. And he didn't try to reassure me anymore. That struck me as wonderful.

And yet I left him. There was some other man, I think, come from the bow of the ship with ice in his drink that had fallen on the deck from the iceberg. My man—what a phrase to come to my lips now, though I mean it only to distinguish him from the other man; I knew neither of their names—my man was quietly disapproving of the other man, who was acting like a fool, it's true, and for a moment, there was a connection between us—my man, yes mine, and me—we heard the foolishness of this outsider together, we were of one mind about this. Then the other was gone, and my stiff Englishman who respected me, clearly, was silently watching the sea, aware of me, I knew. And then something collapsed in me, as sudden and rock-heavy as the coal mine in Mingo County. It was too late for me. For this man, as well. For all of us. All these odd and sweet feelings I was having turned then into bitterness. I couldn't bear to look at him anymore. I slipped away without a word. As quietly as the great ship going under. For the *Titanic* was quiet, in its last plunge.

I stand up from this bed in this cold room and I am still wearing my long skirt and my high-necked linen shirtwaist. I wouldn't let them take these clothes from me, though I know I must yield eventually, but these things on my bed seem little more than a shadowed nakedness. I wandered the ship for a long while and I was among other people but I spoke not another word. To my shame, perhaps. I did not look at the others. I was dead already, it seemed to me. Then I found a place where I could stand and watch the sea, with no one nearby. A high place. Near the wheelhouse, I think, and, unintentionally, on a deck with lifeboats. The orchestra was still playing. As time went on, there were sounds of people rushing, crying out. I braced my mind so as not to hear. I stood looking beyond the bow, far into the slick dark sea, lit bright by the moon, and the air was cold and I began to shiver, but only from the cold, I knew, not from fear. I did not fear death.

My father had died the year before. He was a good man. I sat beside him and the bed was so neat all about him, my mother had tucked him in and folded the covers rightly across his chest, a straight, orderly fold, and there were flowers in a vase beside his bed, and his pajama shirt was starched, and she had done all that she knew to do, so she was weeping hard in another room. I sat beside my father and I touched his hand and his breathing was difficult now, but he turned his face to me.

He did not tell me to be brave. He simply said, "I'm proud of you, Margaret."

I laid my cheek against the back of his hand and wept awhile and I knew he would not misinterpret the tears. They were from gratitude, as much as anything else. Then he slept. And I crept from his room and when I woke in the night, from the touch of the doctor's hand, it was to find that my father had left his body.

As I stood on the boat deck of the *Titanic*, I thought of him. I wondered if he'd had as little use for his body as I had for mine. Of course we never spoke of this. But he seemed to understand so much about me, and he slipped quietly away in the dark, and he was always a man of the mind and the mind's energy surely crackled on beyond the body, it never needed the body. All this fluttered about in me as I stood watching the ocean creep onto the bow, and though they were a little disorganized, these thoughts made me feel it would be all right if this night ended for me as it clearly seemed it would. I even decided to go below and lie in my bed and read. There were only a few pages left to the book I was reading about a man married to a shrewish woman and in love with the wife's cousin and instead of touching each other, the two lovers decide to kill themselves. A woman wrote this book, Mrs. Edith Wharton, and there were things she seemed to understand, and it was sad, I thought, that I would not be able to seek her out and speak with her when I reached New York.

I was about to turn and go. But an image held me. The sea had finally crept over the bow of the ship, a thin cover now, and the moon and stars were there and I thought of Venice, and once again I was planning simply to return to my room and read and it was at that moment I heard his voice, the simplest hello.

I turned to him. His eyes were clearer in the glare of the electric light from the bridge and even the harshness of Mr. Edison's illumination could not take away the softness there.

"I was about to go below and read," I said.

"Nonsense," he said. "You've known all the while what's happening. You must go into a lifeboat now."

"I don't know why," I said. These words came to my lips as quickly as an urge to kiss. This was an act of intimacy, I felt that right away, to tell this man I did not wish to live anymore. I didn't fully understand the feeling myself, really.

I didn't even know how long I'd had it, perhaps only a few moments, perhaps years. And, of course, in that context, he could easily have taken it another way. Not as an independent feeling in me but as an expression of the hopelessness of the situation aboard the *Titanic,* for hopeless it was. But dear God, he knew what I meant. Instantly. He knew my heart. I know he knew. And there was only one answer for him to give, a wildly impertinent answer, an answer only a lover could give, and he spoke it to me. I told him I did not know why I should live and he said, "Because I ask you to."

I wanted to say yes I will live, yes, I will receive this desire from you and perhaps in so doing I'll even apprehend at last what that actually means, to live, for this body of mine must surely have something more to do with it than I've so far discerned. And I was quite acutely aware of my body at that moment, though I could not have said what part, and his eyes held me and he seemed very calm. I was intensely aware of him, the physical presence of him, and then I realized he had changed from his tweeds into a tuxedo. Regrettably, this was an easier thing to speak of.

"You've dressed up," I said.

"To see you off," he said.

I don't think I spoke another word to him after that. Words are the language of the mind, aren't they? Perhaps not for Mrs. Edith Wharton or some others. But for me. He had dressed up to see me off, he had adorned his body for the occasion of offering me life, and I took that life from him, accepted it as I would a kiss from him or a caress or more, and so the language of my mind failed me. And I find

myself now walking around and around this room at the end
of the twentieth century and I am frantic with regret, for
on that night I could find no other language with which to
speak. My hand moved, it's true, my right hand rose as if by
its own intent and it came out toward him and I ached to
put that hand on some part of his body, to touch him—it is
my ache now, too—touch his hand, at least, perhaps even
his cheek, but I could not. Instead my hand found his white
tie, slightly askew, and I straightened it, the gesture of a wife
of many years with her husband, just before going out the
front door of our town house and into a carriage and off to
a play or an opera and he is always doing this, tying his tie
and leaving it crooked, and it's touching, really, for me, for
his wife, because his mind, which respects me and listens to
me and considers me its equal, is so often filled with ideas
that he neglects his body, even in the tying of a white tie
around his neck.

I straightened his tie and my hand was trembling, but
its will was weak, or perhaps simply unpracticed, and it fell
once more beside me, though neither it nor I wanted that,
and he said, "Please hurry."

And if I were the woman my mind had always aspired to
and even believed I was, I should have taken the initiative
there, should have touched him. I should have taken his face
in my two hands and pulled him to me and I should have
kissed him, for there was a kiss yearning on my lips even
then, though at the time I did not clearly recognize it for
what it was. I can recognize it only now. Nearly a century
later.

I did hurry. I turned and we walked together toward a
lifeboat very nearby. No more than half a dozen steps altogether, and yet I was very conscious of walking with him, a
familiar act, an intimate act, our bodies moving beside each
other, we'd let the carriage go and we were walking down
Broadway and there were bright lights all around and we
were talking about the play, about the flow of Mr. Ibsen's
ideas, and then we were before the boat and a hissing came
from the sky and a pop and suddenly there was orange light
all around, like the lights of Broadway. I looked at him and
I wanted to take him in my arms, but I did not, I could not,
I was being a lady, God forgive me, and I wanted him to
take me in his arms but he did not—though I felt that he
wished to, I felt it on my skin just as I'd felt the presence of
death—but he was being a gentleman.

And he said something to a ship steward and it was this
man's hand who took mine and I was in the boat and I looked
about me and I did not remember stepping in and I turned
to look at my man but he was just then retreating into the
shadows and the lifeboat began to descend and then I was
on the sea in a boat full of women, our lives spared because
of our sex, and I was ashamed, and all I wanted was to be
on that deck beside him, and I sank down and my mind
was empty of all ideas and my body was empty of any intent
and after a while the bow of the *Titanic* disappeared and
the stern lifted up and I did not let myself think where he
might be and as the stern lifted, there came a great and
awful noise from the ship and I realized it was from the
silver and the pianos and the porcelain and the couches

and the chairs and the steamer trunks and the wine bottles and the books—every loose object on the ship was crashing forward and breaking—and then all the lights suddenly blinked into darkness and a last tremendous noise rose, the ship cracking in two, and then the stern settled back for a moment as if it might sail off on its own and I thought of him once more, imagined him on this half-ship, sailing away to safety, but quickly the section began again to rise, a dark shadow against the bright night sky, and this time there was a terrible silence. No. There were voices all around, in the water, crying out. But from where I sensed him to be, there was only silence. The stern stood upright for what felt like a very long time and then it began to slide quietly downward, disappearing, faster, faster, and it was gone, and I might as well have been beside him, for I dropped at once into a sleep as dreamless as death.

And have I truly awakened, even now? I stand motionless in the center of this room. There is no sound, except the soft slip of the air. Perhaps I died in the very moment he did. Perhaps this is the purgatory I've been assigned to for my betrayal, a place to show me that the words must be made flesh.

I feel the weight of my clothes upon me and the burden of my breath. It is many years too late but I unfasten my dress and I slip from it and from all the layers of garments beneath, I shed them quickly, tearing at them, throwing them aside, and at last I am standing naked, and I call to him, I cast the words of my mind out to the distant sea. Look at me, I say.

I stand for a long while in the center of this room, praying that his spirit has found its way to me and is gazing on this vessel of my body, bright with lights and holding him.

I am no longer afraid. I move in my nakedness to this other room and I bend to the tub and by my own hands now I let the water rush in and soon this hard white sea is filled and I step in. The water is cold. It takes my breath away. No matter. I sit and it rises up my thighs, my hips, my sides, and it is over my breasts, and it is beneath my chin, and it ripples there, like kisses. He is nearby. I slide quietly beneath the water. I will find him and we will touch.